His Protective Wings

Stones Creek
Ladies of Sanctuary House

Sophie Dawson

May your life be a story in faithful living.

Dedication

Carolyn Leggo has been my editor for many books now. She is dedicated, efficient, knows her grammar and where I need to put commas. She has become a friend as well as my editor. I dedicate this book to her.

Disclaimer

This is a work of fiction. Most of the places within the story are fictitious, but some are real. You will most likely recognize those which are. Those you don't are made up by me. The people, unless you recognize the name of a real historical person, are not real. They, too, have been created by me or by my friend and author George McVey. This is true of Nugget Nate and Penny Ryder, who may or may not show up in this book. Even if real historical people are mentioned, their lives may or may not adhere strictly to documented historical reference. In other words, what they do or say has little bearing in fact and they probably didn't do or say it. This is a fictional story after all.

All Scripture is quoted from the World English Bible.

CHAPTER ONE

Stones Creek, Colorado
November 1868

Ruth Naylor knew she was being watched. She could feel it. She had been aware of it for several weeks. The sensation sent chills up her spine. As much as she told herself it was nonsense to think some man was watching her, Ruth couldn't shake the feeling. With several of the Ladies who lived at Sanctuary House marrying and moving out, taking their children with them, her childcare duties were reduced. That meant she had to find a different source of income. That meant dealing with and going to meet with men.

Ruth stood on the porch of Sanctuary House and looked across the street at the carpenter shop. Arty Massot, the growly carpenter who built most of the buildings in Stones Creek, had approached her last Sunday after worship service and said he'd heard she was looking for cleaning jobs. It was true, she was. The thought of going into a man's living quarters to clean tied her stomach in knots. It also seemed to have nailed her boots to the floorboards of the porch. But she needed the job.

Ruth pried her feet from where they seemed to be fastened and descended the steps. With determination, she walked across the street, to the door of the carpentry shop. Should she knock, or go right in? It was a place of business after all. Lifting her trembling hand, Ruth forced herself to turn the knob and open the door.

The smell of sawdust was thick in Ruth's nostrils. Every surface including the floor had a covering of the stuff. There were partially completed projects around the room with plenty of space to work around each one. Massot was sanding the top of a table, his back toward her.

Ruth studied the piece he was working on. It was unusual. Rather than a rectangle, square or circle, the table's edges were irregular. She realized the top was made from a cross section cut from the trunk of a huge tree. The concentric circles of the growth rings created a beautiful design on its surface. To have dried the wood in such a way that it didn't split from the edge to the center spoke of the skill and knowledge of the carpenter polishing the table with such care.

Several other pieces of furniture were unusual, also. There were two small end-tables made in a similar fashion as the large one with a cross section cut as the top. The legs were made of wood bent in 'U'-shapes. Two partially assembled chairs were being built in the same manner; the frame made from trunks or branches of trees.

Massot turned around and jerked, startled to see Ruth standing just inside the door. "Oh, Miss Naylor, forgive me. I didn't realize you had come in. I get lost in my work." His low raspy voice sent shivers down Ruth's spine, doing strange things to her middle.

"I'm sorry. Should I have knocked?" Ruth twisted her fingers together.

Massot stepped forward. "No, of course not. This is a place of business. Anyone can come right in during business hours."

Ruth nodded. "I— um, you— um, mentioned you were looking for someone to clean your living quarters." She glanced around the messy workspace. It could use a good cleaning too, though she would never say so.

He must have noticed her perusal. "I know. This place is filthy, also. I've been very busy building houses and furniture. There hasn't been time to shovel it out." He gave a slight kick to the thick layer of sawdust trampled on the floor.

Ruth didn't know what to say, so she said nothing, waiting for him to speak.

"Come, I'll show you what I'd like you to clean." He moved to the staircase along the back wall. She was surprised, since there was an exterior one on the side of the building, also. Not many had both.

Following him up the steps, Ruth found both sets shared the same landing. Massot opened the door and entered his living area. He cleared his throat. "As you can see, I'm in desperate need of help."

That was an understatement. The room they entered was a parlor of sorts. Or maybe it was more accurate to say the space they entered was the parlor. It appeared the entire upstairs of the building was one large open space with a sitting area or parlor near the stairs. To the far right were stacks of lumber seemingly sorted by type of wood and sizes of boards.

Behind the seating space was a large cookstove, cabinets, and a small table with two chairs. Further on, along the front of the building was a bed, dresser, and washstand. The only completely walled section was directly behind the stove. Stud walls divided the other areas. It was as if he'd stopped working on the apartment before doing the lath and plaster to complete the walls.

Plus, the place was a mess. Sawdust was tracked everywhere. It also covered most surfaces. Brown paper, articles of clothing, books, newspapers, tools, rolls of paper she thought might be blueprints were scattered all over. The windows were covered with sawdust and grime, as were the exterior walls.

The room was surprisingly warm for such a large open space. Ruth wondered how that could be but didn't ask. Massot had told her it was a disaster and he didn't know where to start. Ruth barely did herself.

"Miss Naylor, as you can see, I'm in desperate need of someone to make order out of this chaos and to keep it up. I'm sick of living in such a mess but don't have the time, knowledge, or inclination to do the work it will take to do so. I'm willing to pay well for you to do the initial cleaning and then pay a fair wage for your continued services." The amount he offered wiped away the doubts she had of working in the man's home. Or, at least she was willing to put them aside until he broke what little trust she had in any man.

"Yes, this place could stand for a strong wind to blow through to get most of the evidence of your job sent out the window. Since it's the end of November, that's not possible. I don't think opening the windows is such a good idea in this cold weather."

"Then, you'll take the project on?" Massot's hopeful tone almost brought a smile to Ruth's lips.

"Where will you be while I clean?" she asked.

"Not up here. I'll either be working downstairs or on a house here in town. With winter coming, I'll be here more often than in the warmer weather. I won't come up when you are here, so long as you let me know when you arrive. I'd appreciate you telling me when you finish, also."

"Since you'll pay me when I leave, I most certainly will tell you when I leave, as well as when I come."

Massot grinned at her. "Thank you. Do you want to start today?"

"I'll need to go back to the house and change into my work clothes."

"Thank you, Miss Naylor. You are a Godsend. I was about ready to chuck everything out a window and start over."

Ruth descended the exterior staircase, leaving Massot to go down the interior back to his shop. She'd heard that he was grumpy and growly from others living in and around Stones Creek, but she'd not seen that side of him. Anytime he spoke with her, Massot had been unfailingly polite. Now, she just needed to conquer her unease at being in the building while he was the only other person on the premises.

Ruth walked across to Sanctuary House willing her stomach to unclench. Men, especially the attentions of men, made Ruth extremely nervous. Twelve years ago, a prominent businessman had stalked Ruth for months. Being only seventeen and innocent, she hadn't been aware of it. One day, saying he had gotten in a special order he thought she might like, the man trapped her in the back room of his store. What occurred there, Ruth didn't want to think about. When she told her parents what had happened to her, they hadn't believed her. The rape left Ruth with child. She'd been kicked out of her family as a soiled woman and a liar.

Ruth had walked to the next town carrying what little she could pack in a carpet bag and the few dollars she'd earned from selling eggs. Hoping to find some kind of work, Ruth had found something better.

A tall mountain man, dressed in dirty buckskins and his well-dressed, dignified wife seemed to have been waiting for her. As Ruth walked up Main Street, the man strode up to her and said, "I'm a believin' you's the gal we's a been waitin' fer, my Penny 'an me. I done had me a Callin' 'bout a young woman whose been dealt with mighty poorly. Since I don't rightly knowst why any lady as young as yer be should be a wanderin' inta town with only a carpet bag an' a sorrowful face, you be the one, I's sure. Penny, m'love. I done found her. Reckon we kin be a headin' ta Sanctuary Place now."

Ruth had just stared at him. How could he know she'd been unjustly accused and found guilty when she was the victim of a heinous act? She'd backed away, slowly. She'd heard about men who tried to lure women by promising them aid. Instead, they often ended up in brothels selling themselves, receiving only pennies while the brothel owner kept the majority of the fee charged.

It had taken Penny Ryder, beloved wife of the famous Nugget Nate Ryder, to convince Ruth the offer of help was genuine. After buying her a meal in the local café, the journey across Wisconsin had begun. They ended up in Iowa at the mission for women called Sanctuary Place that was sponsored by the couple. It was where Ruth's daughter, Kathryn, was born eleven years ago.

In July, eight Ladies had arrived in Stones Creek, Colorado. They'd come to Nugget Nate's new Sanctuary House to begin new lives and possibly find husbands in the women-starved West. Ruth didn't necessarily want a husband, but the opportunity for a new start for herself and her daughter lured her to join the Ladies moving to Colorado.

The goal was for them to find husbands but each woman had to find jobs to support themselves in the meantime. Ruth had been tending the children of the other Ladies living in Sanctuary House while they worked. With several now married and the older children in school, the number she cared for during the day had dwindled. Ruth now needed additional work to supplement her income.

Ruth had been offered the job of cleaning the general store owned by Ben Cutler when he and his family moved into the house Massot was building for them. It would be finished shortly and the move would take place before Christmas. Sara, Ben's wife, had asked Ruth to begin cleaning now since she was in an interesting condition and not feeling well much of the time.

The cleaning jobs would have to be done after the Ladies whose children Ruth watched came home from their jobs. That meant she would be doing the cleaning on Saturdays or in the evenings. It wasn't ideal as Ruth didn't like the thought of being in the buildings alone at night. She wasn't pleased with the prospect of walking back to the House in the dark either. At the moment, it couldn't be helped. Massot wanting her to work on Saturdays eased those concerns, but having to be alone with him in the building brought others to mind.

~~~~~

She's a shy little thing. Doesn't talk much either, Massot thought as he went back to polishing the table. He chuckled to himself. It wasn't as if he was very talkative either. He rubbed his throat. Too much talking made it hurt. The bullet that winged his throat during the war had left him with a gravelly voice and limited his desire to talk. He knew people thought he was a taciturn old goat, and maybe that was partly true, but his throat just kept him from making small talk.

Arty Massot had come to Stones Creek when it was first settled. He'd built most of the buildings in the town. Owned a few too. That was seventeen years ago, when he was just twenty-one. Part of the Code of the West was not to ask anyone why they came west and Massot honored that and appreciated that others did too. His stint in the Union army was the only time he'd left Stones Creek for more than a few days at a time when he traveled to Denver to get carpentry supplies.

Miss Naylor was also pretty. She was petite and slender. She'd fit him well if he were to hold her against him since he wasn't overly tall. Where did that thought come from? She wouldn't be interested in him. He was just a carpenter and wasn't looking for a wife.

He knew she had a daughter. What was her name? Kathryn, he thought. She was one of the older children who had come to Sanctuary House with their mothers last July.

Eight women had moved into the large house Massot had helped build for Nugget Nate Ryder. They'd come from Sanctuary Place Mission for Women, hoping to start new lives and possibly find husbands. Nugget Nate had set up a council of four respected men in town to approve any man who wanted to court the Ladies. He didn't want the Ladies to end up married to men who might abuse them in some way.

Massot ran a hand across the table top. Soon, he'd be able to varnish it. He picked up the block of wood he'd fastened sandpaper onto and checked the paper. He'd have to change it soon.

Hearing the shop door open, Massot turned around. Miss Naylor entered carrying a broom. She'd changed her gown. This one was an ugly brown only fit for the job she was going to be doing. She had a black wool shawl around her shoulders, hugging it to herself with one hand.

"Um, do you have a bucket I can put trash and sweepings in?" she asked, biting her bottom lip.

Massot chuckled. "Ma'am, you'll need more than a bucket. Let me get you a barrel. You fill it up and I'll dispose of what you collect."

"Thank you." She broke eye contact and hurried to the stairs and, picking up her skirts, she climbed them as Massot watched. She paused at the landing and looked down at him. It was dim so he couldn't see clearly, but he thought her eyes widened with worry before she opened the door and entered his apartment.

She's a scared little thing, too.

Massot got his scrap barrel and took it outside to

dump on his burn pile behind the building. No sense taking the half-filled thing upstairs. Lifting it onto his shoulder, he climbed the stairs and entered the apartment. Miss Naylor jumped a bit when he opened the door.

"Oh, yes, thank you," she said, her hand fluttering nervously.

"I'll just put it here and leave you to your work. If you get it filled before you leave, let me know and I'll empty it for you." Massot set it down at the end of the settee where she'd already swept. Several piles of sweepings were scattered around the seating area.

"Th...thank you." She had stepped back when he moved forward into the room.

"I'll head back down to the shop. If you need anything, just let me know."

"I...I will. Thank you."

Massot shook his head as he descended the stairs. Miss Naylor certainly was nervous around him. Maybe she was just scared of men in general. Thinking about the times he'd noticed her at church or town events, he realized she seldom spoke to men or even stood near one. The fact that she was Miss Naylor and had a daughter meant she'd been with a man pretty intimately at least once. Maybe that was why she was so nervous around men.

The thought sickened Massot. He didn't know her story and would never ask. He respected the privacy of the Ladies just as the Code of the West dictated. Besides, it was none of his business anyway.

Massot knew some of the town's folk didn't approve of the Ladies. They considered them beneath themselves. Massot thought it was the other way around. The Ladies were devout in their faith and were raising their children in the Lord. Sure, the boys, especially, were prone to mischief but it was never destructive or mean. He could think of some of the children in town who were, and they were from those 'fine, upstanding' citizens who looked down their noses at the Ladies and their offspring.

Looking over his shop from the bottom step, he decided it might be time to clean it up a bit. Sure, he could sweep up, but Miss Naylor needed the work. Besides, he wondered if she would be able to do the work with him in the same room. Not that he wanted to scare her. He grinned. But she was a pretty thing. Maybe they could get to know one another a little. Not that he was interested in courting her. No, she might be looking for a husband, and Massot was sure he'd never be someone she would be interested in. He was just a carpenter, not a doctor, lawyer, or banker who a woman would want as a husband.

Moving to the table, Massot picked up the sanding block and began smoothing the table.

CHAPTER TWO

"His place was the dirtiest place I've ever seen," Ruth said. It was late evening and the children were in bed. The Ladies were gathered in the parlor, each doing some kind of needlework. They were knitting or crocheting. Hats and gloves or mittens were being made to give the children for Christmas which was about a month away.

"He'd tracked sawdust up and left I don't know how many newspapers scattered on the floor. And the walls aren't even built. Just a couple. Mostly it's just studs. I don't know how he can live like that."

"Men can live in a pig pen." Chloe Ashburn drew some more yarn from the ball in her work basket. Her knitting needles clacked softly as she stitched. "I've only been up in McIlroy's room a few times after Dunc shot him, but his place was a mess too. Pastor Noah did dishes while I picked up clothing and rags and other wash on the floor." Chloe's son had accidentally shot the blacksmith in the behind. They were now engaged and would be marrying just before the holidays.

Laura Duffle laughed. "He was one of the men who wanted to wait weeks before they brought in extremely dirty laundry for me to wash." Laura's laundry business was quite successful since most of the town and surrounding area was populated with single men. "They all learned it's better to bring them regularly since I charge more for extra dirty laundry. A lot more."

Blanche Basking, the unofficial leader of Sanctuary House, cut the yarn and held up the finished mitten. "Three down and five more mittens to go. I'll be tired of mittens by the time I get all my children's ones done." She had four children, three boys and one girl.

"I'll help. I'm nearly done with Kathryn's things." Ruth held up the hat she was crocheting. "I should finish this tonight or tomorrow."

"You're a sweetheart, Ruth. I'll take you up on the offer."

These four ladies were those still living at the House. The other four had married and were living in town or elsewhere nearby. The ladies who moved to Stones Creek were expected to work to make their own living until they married. If they never did, they were welcome to stay at Sanctuary House as long as they wanted while supporting themselves and any children by working. Chloe would move out when she and McIlroy married. She would take her two children with her.

Blanche and Chloe had started a cafe partnering with Almeda Wilson, an ex-slave who ran a bakery. She had combined it with the cafe and all three ran it for two meals a day, six days a week. Laura had her laundry business which was supporting her and her two boys.

"Massot asked if I'd help him clean his shop once I have the upstairs done." Ruth chuckled. "The sawdust must be a couple of inches thick on the floor and every surface. You can tell where he's worked last because it's cleared off there."

"Are you going to?" Laura asked.

"Yes, next Friday afternoon once Blanche comes back from the café. Without any other children but Lil-Pen and John, I'm free in the afternoons. Almeda picks up Abraham in late morning."

"That's true," Blanche said. "Are you going to try and find other businesses to clean?"

"I hope to. I'm afraid they'll want me to clean at night after they close. I don't want to work in an empty building at night, but I need the work. Cleaning the store and Massot's apartment won't earn enough for me and Kathryn. Next year John will start school so that will leave me with only Almeda's Abe."

The Ladies nodded their understanding. Before all the weddings there had been enough children for Ruth to mind. School took all of those old enough to attend and the marriages had taken the younger ones she had watched.

Ruth set her crocheting aside. Her situation discouraged her. "I'm going up to bed. I'll see you all tomorrow." She rose and left the room. Her friends watched her go with sympathy in their eyes. They understood how difficult it was for Ruth to be near a man, let alone speak with one.

~~~~~

Stepping down off the step of the church onto the snow sprinkled grass, Ruth saw Massot striding away. He was heading off into the woods. He did that nearly every Sunday. Always alone. She wondered if he had memories he wanted to mull over or if he simply liked to walk in the woods.

Massot had spoken a few words to her before service, telling her what a good job she'd done cleaning his flat. Ruth knew she'd turned bright red at the praise as her cheeks had heated, making her want to press her gloved hands to them. She hadn't, of course. That would have given away that his words had affected her more than they should have.

Ruth couldn't remember the last time a man had praised her. Probably her father before he banished her. Then again, he hadn't been one who complimented anyone very often. He'd rather be judgmental. Knowing how that felt, Ruth praised Kathryn often wanting her to grow up to be confident and self-assured.

"Miss Naylor?"

Ruth turned and saw Mr. and Mrs. Ritter standing behind her. Mr. CJ Ritter was president of Stones Creek National Bank. Mrs. Debbie Ritter was petite with a wide smile. She was friendly to everyone in town. Ruth had heard that she and Mrs. Norie Pierce, daughter of the owner of the Chasing R Ranch, were best of friends.

"Good morning, Mr. Ritter, Mrs. Ritter." Ruth waited. There must be something they wanted as they'd never singled her out before.

"I've been hearing from Ben Cutler and Arty Massot how well you've been cleaning their places. I was up in Massot's apartment and was very impressed. I've been up there before and the difference is astounding."

Ruth suppressed the grin pulling at her lips. Yes, Massot's place did look much better but she didn't want to seem proud.

"I'm looking for someone to clean the bank. Since Birdie Putnam married Harvey Hayes, I haven't had anyone making sure the bank is cleaned on a regular basis. Would you be interested in taking on the job?"

Ruth glanced at Mrs. Ritter who smiled encouragingly. "Um, when would you want me to do the cleaning?" Her stomach tightened thinking she'd have to work at night and walk both ways in the dark.

Mr. Ritter answered. "My suggestion would be Wednesday afternoon as the bank closes at twelve o'clock."

A smile came as she heard his suggestion. "That would work well, Mr. Ritter. It would need to be after Blanche, Mrs. Basking, comes from the cafe. I watch her son while she's at work."

"That will be fine. I normally work a few hours in the afternoon, so I can let you in." Mr. Ritter shook Ruth's hand, then said, "I won't take up any more of your Sunday. I'll see you on Wednesday. Just knock on the door when you arrive and I'll let you in."

"Thank you, Mr. Ritter, Mrs. Ritter. I appreciate the work. I'll do a good job."

"I'm sure you will," Mr. Ritter said as he guided his wife away.

Ruth glanced around, seeing her daughter, Kathryn, and several of the other House children walking toward home. It was those who had chores for the noon meal. Laura Duffle was with them. It was her meal to get ready to serve. The other children were still running around the church yard playing with some of Stones Creek's children. She wondered how long it would take her to just see them all as the town's children rather than separate groups.

"What were the Ritters speaking with you about?" Blanche placed a hand on Ruth's arm as she stepped up.

Ruth smiled. "God does provide. Mr. Ritter asked me to clean the bank. It's not going to be much, but it's another income, and I can work during the afternoon."

"Yes, He does. I'm so glad for you." They began walking away from the church. Blanche linked her arm with Ruth's.

"I still need more income, but I'm trusting that He will supply all my needs."

"I'm sure He will," Blanche said. "Come along children," she called and those of the House came running.

~~~~~

December was active with two of the King gang attempting to kidnap Chloe Ashburn but ending up in jail. Then her marriage to McIlroy, and she, Duncan, and Lil-Pen moving out of the House.

All the Ladies, both married and single, with the exception of Esther Fuller who'd left town with her trapper husband, had gathered at the House to celebrate Christmas dinner. Now, Ruth held a weeping Kathryn on her bed.

"I ruined the whole play. But that cow pooping and peeing right next to me. I just couldn't sit there. It stunk so much. Everyone will hate me."

Ruth fought the giggle that threatened to escape her lips. "No one will hate you. I understand why you ran out."

"But they'll never want me to be Mary again," Kathryn sobbed, clinging to her mother. "And I knew every line I was supposed to say."

"Mr. Bergdorf knows that. I'm sure he'll take that into consideration when they plan the play for next year." Ruth patted her back. "You certainly were a memorable Mary."

Ozzie Basking stuck his head in the room. "I wish I'd been on the stage when that cow pooped. That would have been so great."

"Ma's not happy that poop and pee got on her dressing gown." Will Basking could be heard in the hall. "I told them the kings shouldn't have to wear ladies clothes just 'cause they look like rich people clothes." Both boys ran on to their room.

Kathryn had stopped sobbing when the first boy spoke. She let out a small giggle. "They did look stupid in the gowns. All the ruffles and lace."

CHAPTER THREE

The Ladies stood on the platform of the railroad station waiting for the train. A telegram had been received a few days before that two more ladies from Sanctuary Place were coming right after the New Year: Gema Volkovichna and Libby Trembly.

They knew Gema. She had come to Sanctuary Place at the age of sixteen when her family died of influenza as they immigrated from Russia while traveling through Iowa. She hadn't known any English at the time and still struggled with the language. She was now twenty. Libby Trembly no one knew. They were curious why the two women had been sent across the prairie in the dead of winter.

A whistle, clatter and rumble, along with the whoosh of steam brought the train to the station. Ira Bragg, the station master and telegraph operator, came out of the building. He was short and thin with eyes that bugged out of his face. Stringy blonde hair hung below his hat as he strutted across the platform. "It's twenty-five minutes late," he complained.

Ruth knew that. They'd been standing in the cold since ten minutes before the scheduled arrival. None of the Ladies wanted to wait in the station though it would be warmer. Bragg watched them with his wide buggy eyes. It made Ruth far too nervous.

Gema's call rang across the platform from where she stood on the steps of the rail car waiting for the conductor to place the steps. "Myra, Cora, Ruth, Chloe, Blanche, Laura."

Ruth smiled. Gema was just as vivacious as ever. She by-passed the steps, jumping down as soon as the conductor was out of the way. Soon, she was hugging each of her friends, letting out a string of broken English in her excitement.

Glancing up, Ruth saw another young woman descend the steps. There was an aura of deep sadness surrounding her. She went to identify all the baggage being unloaded. This must be Libby Trembly. It was odd that she be sent to Sanctuary House so soon from when she'd arrived there. She couldn't have been there more than a few months as Ruth and the others had come to Stones Creek in July.

"Miss Naylor?"

Ruth turned swiftly toward the male voice. Ira Bragg stood behind her. He was looking her up and down.

"Yes, Mr. Bragg?"

"I've heard you do cleaning. I'm needing someone to clean the station. Not real good at it myself."

"Oh?" Ruth didn't want to take the job. The man made her far too nervous. "When would you want it done?"

"I'm thinking Tuesday evenings. That's one of my nights to man the station and telegraph."

"I see." There was no way Ruth was going to be in the station alone with that man at night. It gave her the willies just thinking about it.

"Ruth, come." Gema grabbed her in a hug. "We go now. Want see House. Can't wait."

With relief, Ruth turned from the weaselly man and followed the rest of the Ladies away from the station. Gema was bouncing with excitement as they walked along the boardwalk, passing Cutler General Store.

Ruth trailed slightly behind walking slowly with Libby Trembly. "I'm Ruth Naylor. You must be Libby. I'm pleased to meet you. Welcome to Stones Creek and Sanctuary House."

"Thank you. Pleased to meet you too." Libby gave a weak smile that didn't reach her eyes. Ruth got the impression Libby didn't really care where she was. She decided to become the sad woman's good friend.

~~~~~

Massot looked up as Hank Johnson came into his workshop. Early March had been horrible for Stones Creek. A measles epidemic was sweeping through the area keeping Massot busy building caskets. He set down the plane he was smoothing with.

His stomach tightened. Ruth's face came to mind. He hadn't heard that she'd taken ill, but Kathryn had. Hank's face told him he'd be building another casket. Massot swallowed waiting for Hank to tell him who had died.

"We need a coffin for Lucy Tanner. She passed last night."

Sorrow and relief fought within him. "Those poor babes. First, their pa is killed by those outlaws. Now, they've lost their ma."

"Yeah. Lucy gave the twins to Libby Trembly to raise. They'd gotten real close." Hank let out a tired breath. "Lucy just gave up. Laura said she never got over her husband's death."

"You've been a real blessing to the House, Hank. All you've done for the Ladies and children." Massot picked up the plane and began running it over the wood again. "How long do I need to make the casket for Lucy?" Hank relayed the information, patted Massot on the shoulder and left.

Massot let the relief he felt that it wasn't Ruth or Kathryn he was building for flood through him. Not that he was going to act on his attraction to Miss Naylor. There was no way she would want him. He was just a carpenter after all. Just a man who worked with his hands instead of a lawyer or banker or business man.

He looked around his workshop. In early January he'd asked Ruth to clean it. It had taken several days to get most of the scraps and sawdust cleared out. Then they had arranged his tools, creating permanent places for each one. That had been her idea. It certainly helped knowing where they were when he needed one. That is, if he remembered to put it back when he was finished. He was getting better at that. Or had been before the epidemic struck. Now the place was inches deep in sawdust and scraps again and his tools were scattered around. Once the rush of caskets needed was over maybe he'd ask her to help him again.

~~~~~

Ruth looked down at the girl sleeping beside Kathryn. Nancy Basking slept in the trundle bed nearby. The evidence of tears traced down Mae's face. What was going to happen next in Stones Creek? First, the epidemic, then Gema was kidnapped by outlaws. By the grace of God, she'd escaped and been found by Red Dickerson.

When they made it back to town, Gema told enough details about where she'd been held that a posse was sent out hoping to capture the criminal gang haunting the area. The posse hadn't found the outlaws, but rather four abandoned children. They were in the process of burying a fifth. Brought to Sanctuary House, the children were taken in, bathed, fed, accepted as the precious ones they were in the eyes of God.

Boone was the oldest and looked to be around twelve. The other boy, Tadpole claimed to be eight. Nina, a little girl the others said was three, had wide eyes that flickered with fear, joy, and longing as her life changed so drastically in one day.

The one Ruth watched sleeping was Mae. At only ten, she'd been raped by the men of the gang and was suffering the aftermath of that. Ruth understood. So did Chloe McIlroy who had been kidnapped and raped at about the same age as Mae, living with the gang until they'd abandoned her and her son Duncan when she was about to give birth to Lil Pen.

"Is she sleeping quietly?" The soft voice of Blanche had Ruth turning her head to see her friend standing in the doorway.

Ruth stepped back and they went into the hallway. "Yes, she seems to be. The depravity of man. To do such evil to one so young."

"I know. At least now they can know the love and security they've missed their entire lives. Duncan shows that a child can overcome that sort of beginning. We'll pray that we can help do the same for these young ones."

"How are the boys and Nina?"

"Nina's sleeping in with the twins and seems to be doing well. She cried for her mama for a while. Boone said she has every night since the adults all left. He and Tadpole thought they were sleeping on the floor in the spare room on the third floor. They didn't think they would have a bed. It just breaks my heart." Blanche's eyes were nearly overflowing.

Ruth patted her friend on the shoulder. "I'm so thankful they were rescued and brought here. We can do just like they do at Sanctuary Place back in Iowa. Tend to their physical needs and help the Lord tend their spiritual ones."

"Amen."

Ruth and Blanche made their way to their own beds, each praying for wisdom and strength to deal with the challenges of the four abandoned children.

CHAPTER FOUR

Spring began peeking its head as tulips and daffodils emerged that the ladies had planted around the foundation of the House in the fall. Massot sat looking out the window of his flat. Below Ruth and her daughter, Kathryn, were planting seeds in the space he'd plowed up for a garden. Ruth had asked him if the Ladies of the House could plant a garden beside his workshop. They would give him all the fresh vegetables he wanted and supply him with canned produce as they processed it.

Kathryn, though only eleven, seemed to have experience with gardening. She was working in one row and Ruth in another.

Grinning, Massot remembered the day he and Ruth had been working to clean his workshop. Kathryn had come in after school and thrown herself in her mother's arms. Though she wasn't crying, she was obviously upset.

"I hate that Junior Brook. He's mean and no one likes him. He called me a bad name. Then Dunc and Ozzie started hitting him, which made me feel better, but they all got in trouble and everybody looked at me.

No one would play with me after school. Well, the House girls would but the town girls wouldn't."

Ruth put her arms around Kathryn. It seemed she didn't know what to say. With no father and her mother being Miss Naylor, Massot knew what Junior had called her. He also knew that Mr. and Mrs. Brooks didn't approve of any of the Ladies or their children. They also didn't like that the Wilsons, who were ex-slaves, lived in Stones Creek.

Kathryn was a pretty girl who would grow into a beautiful young woman. Even better, she was willing to help Ruth with her work. She often helped Ruth clean his flat on Saturdays. Massot had purchased a handful of hair ribbons and given them to her as a thank you. Kathryn had been surprised, giving him a big hug and huge smile. He still remembered the tightening of his heart and the thought that if he had a daughter, he'd want her to be just like Kathryn.

His gaze went to Ruth. Swallowing down his desire for her, Massot turned away from the window. There was no sense wanting what he couldn't have. He didn't have anything to offer a woman and child.

~~~~~

Ruth held Nina's hand and led Boone, Tadpole, and Mae across the street from the House to the garden. Since the children had never been to a school, Ruth decided to give the three older ones lessons at the House. Each morning they spent several hours learning their letters and numbers as well as their assigned chores.

Today, they were going to learn to weed. Not trusting they wouldn't pull the seedlings, the children would be pulling plants from the footpaths. Setting each to their own row, Ruth knelt to pick the grass from around the vegetable shoots. Nina played in the dirt around the edge of the garden.

A shiver went up her spine. She looked left and right surreptitiously not wanting to alert the children to her distress or whomever might be watching her. Not seeing anyone, Ruth turned around to weed the row behind her. As she picked around the seedlings, she took subtle glances, trying not to move her head from side to side. A shadow moved within the trees behind the garden and workshop. Or did it? Was she imagining things, or was there truly someone in the woods?

Ruth reached for another weed. Her hand shook. Her fingers fumbled, unable to close around the blade of grass. *Please, Lord, don't let it be someone watching me. I don't think I could handle it. Please take this fear from me. Fear is not of You. I am covered by Your feathers and find refuge under Your wings. Thank You for Your protection.* Ruth made the words of Psalm 91:4 her own in her prayer. She allowed the peaceful security of the verse to flow over her and let out a soft breath.

"Miss Ruth," Nina said, running up the row. "Look what I found." She held out a grimy hand. "It's a worm."

Ruth smiled. "Yes, it certainly is. How about you put it right down here? Watch what he does." She pointed right next to the pea plant seedlings. Nina dropped the dirt speckled worm.

"Ooo. Look, he's digging right down in."

"Yes. Worms help open up the soil so the plants can grow."

John Basking ran up then. He was five but hadn't

been allowed to come with them to the garden since he'd gotten into a fight with his brother Will before the older children left for school. "Laura says it's time for lunch. You're to come home and wash up without touching anything with your mucky hands, especially the napkins. She just finished ironing them."

Ruth took one more look around, allowing the children to run across the street. The feeling of being watched had faded but the effect lingered. Her shoulders shuddered as she stepped onto the walk leading to the House.

~~~~~

"He's supposed to get here next week." CJ Ritter sat down at his desk as Ruth finished dusting the small table between the two straight chairs in his office. Ruth was nearly done cleaning the bank. She always did the bank president's office last. By that time Mr. Ritter was nearly finished working for the day and inclined to talk.

"What's the lawyer's name? I forget," Ruth asked.

CJ smiled. "Forsyth Franklin Fredrick Farnsworth the Fourth."

"Oh my. That's a mouthful."

He chuckled. "That's something I'm familiar with. You know my given name, don't you?"

"No, I don't believe I've ever heard you called anything but Mr. Ritter or CJ."

"I was christened Chalmers Jehoshaphat Ritter. That's why I go by CJ. I'm thinking we may need to figure out a nickname for Forsyth Franklin Fredrick Farnsworth the Fourth."

Ruth grinned. "Might be best. He'd be teased pretty fiercely with that name."

Ruth completed her work, said goodbye, and left the bank. She crossed the street and walked between Pastor Preston's gun shop and Leah Steele's dressmaker shop. As she turned into the alley behind the House, Ira Bragg stepped in front of her.

Ruth jumped back a step. Her heart began to pound. "Mr. Bragg, you startled me. What are you doing behind the House?"

Ira stuck out his leg, pointing his toe to the side, his hand on his hip. His oily blond hair hung in stringy clumps to his shoulders. "I been meaning to speak to you, Miss Naylor." Bug eyes looked her up and down making her feel as if her brown work wrapper was peeling off.

Ruth took a step back. "You have?" The words clogged her throat. She shifted her weight to her other foot, moving away from him slightly as he leaned toward her.

"Yes, ma'am." Ira took another step, following her movement. "Been watching and decided you're a pretty enough woman. I'm a wantin' to come a courtin'. Just thought I'd be lettin' you know that. I'm thinkin' we can go out walkin' this comin' Saturday night."

Ruth swallowed. Twice. Three times. "You've gotten permission to court me?"

"That's a dumb idea. I don't need any man tellin' me if I can court some woman. Especially one of you women living in this place." Ira shoved a thumb toward the House.

The contempt in his voice gave Ruth even more confirmation that she'd never accept being courted by Ira Bragg, let alone consider marrying him. It was difficult enough for Ruth to think of marrying any man, let alone one who held her in such disrespect.

"Mr. Bragg." Ruth fought to keep the tremors surging through her from her voice. "Don't bother coming to the House on Saturday. I will not, then nor ever, go walking with you or allow myself to be courted by you. It's obvious you have no respect for me or for Nugget Nate Ryder since he is the one who set up the rules for the men who want to court us. Leave me alone and no one will hear of this conversation. Approach me again, and I'll make sure all the men of the committee know." Ruth tried to brush past him but he grabbed her arm.

"You think you're too good for me? You who had a baby without a husband. You're nothing but a two bit…"

His words were cut off when the back door to Hank Johnson's barber shop opened. Laura Duffle stepped out. Ira dropped his hand from her arm. Hustling by him she called out to her friend. She knew Laura could tell something had happened by the questioning look she gave Ruth.

Once they were in the kitchen, Laura said, "What happened? You're white as a sheet?"

Ruth sat heavily on a chair. "Mr. Bragg told me he was going to court me. Told me he'd been watching and that I was pretty enough for him." A shudder ran through Ruth. He'd been watching her. A shadow of the man who had raped her slid across her mind. He'd watched her too.

Laura's mouth dropped open. "The committee gave him permission to court you?"

"No, he thinks he's too good to ask any man's permission to court a woman like me. He came very close to calling me a name because I had Kathryn without a husband."

Laura's hand flew to her mouth. "Oh my. How insulting. You didn't agree, did you?"

"Of course not. Not only was he disrespectful, he practically undressed me with his eyes. Nothing could persuade me to consider him as a suitor." Ruth rubbed her face with her hands. "Now I just need to push all the bad memories he brought up from where they were buried back into the abyss where they belong."

Laura patted her on the shoulder. "Forget about Mr. Bragg. There's no way the committee would ever give him permission to court any woman. I've seen each of the men give him the stink eye when he looks at us."

Nugget Nate Ryder, who had built and funded Sanctuary House, had chosen four men of Stones Creek to approve any man wanting to court one of the Ladies of the House. Knowing of the backgrounds of the Ladies, he and Penny, his wife, didn't want any to be courted and possibly marry a man of poor character. The committee was composed of Sheriff Newt Riverby, who had married one of the Ladies himself, Dr. Eli Pierce, Pastor Noah Preston, and Ben Cutler, owner of the general store. These men took their job seriously. None of the Ladies knew who was rejected as that information was kept close to their vests.

"Don't tell anyone, please. I don't want all the sympathy chatter. It doesn't help with the memories."

"I won't. But, do you want Hank to keep an eye out for him? I know he would." Laura moved to the stove, stoking the coals to begin preparations for supper.

"I hope it won't be necessary. He keeps pretty busy at the station and monitoring the telegraph."

"I'll ask him anyway, also to not say anything about it."

Ruth smiled her thanks.

CHAPTER FIVE

"Did you hear what happened today with Tadpole?" Libby asked Ruth as she came into the house. She was working at Cutler's General Store several hours a day. Sara Cutler was expecting, and it was more difficult than her previous confinements. She was needing to rest more, so Libby's hours were expanded to cover those Sara could no longer work. This gave added income to Libby and to Ruth who was paid to watch Arleta and Jack Tanner, Libby's foster children. They were now nearly twenty months old.

"No, what happened? I haven't seen him much today. He did his lessons and weeding, then disappeared." Ruth was preparing supper with Blanche.

Libby giggled as she took off her hat. "I shouldn't laugh, but it's so funny. Well, not if you were Traci Fugard. Tadpole doesn't seem to know that you shouldn't just walk into someone's house."

"Oh?" Ruth and Blanche stopped what they were doing and looked at Libby.

"He walked right into the front door of her house and on into the kitchen. Mrs. Fugard was sitting in her bathtub taking a bath. She looked up and there was

41

Tadpole. She screamed and he ran."

"Oh my." Both ladies covered their mouths with their hands in shock.

"She got dressed and stormed into the sheriff's office and told him to arrest Tadpole. Sheriff Riverby said he'd take care of it."

"Is Tadpole in jail?" Ruth started to take off her apron ready to head to the jail to bail him out.

"Not in a jail cell. When he was found, hiding in an empty stall in the livery, Sheriff Riverby took him back to the jail to talk with him. I guess he's not back yet."

Ruth and Blanche looked at one another. Then they looked at Libby. All three burst out laughing.

"Poor Mrs. Fugard. How embarrassing." Blanche was laughing so hard she had to sit down. "But it serves the old biddy right. She's been nothing but disapproving and arrogant since we came to Stones Creek."

A knock sounded on the front door. All three ladies went through the dining room into the entryway. Ruth opened the door to find Sheriff Riverby holding Tadpole by the shoulder. He tipped his hat.

"Sorry to disturb you, ma'am, but this fellow got into a bit of trouble today."

"Come in, Sheriff. Libby was just telling what she'd heard." Ruth looked down at Tadpole whose face showed evidence of tears on his dusty cheeks. "Come here, Tadpole." She held her arms out to him, and he dove into them.

"I didn't mean to cause no trouble. That house looked real friendly like what with all them flowers around the porch. I'm wanting to meet more of the townsfolk. Most been real nice to me and the others."

He turned his face up. Ruth brushed his cheek with her fingers.

"Mrs. Fugard wasn't very appreciative of Tadpole's visit," Sheriff Riverby said, his lips twitching trying not to break into a smile. "He and I've had a little talk about the way things work in town."

"Out of town too," Tadpole piped in. "If I'm gonna be a law 'biding citzen, I gotta r'spect other folk's houses and such. Cain't just go walking in. I gotta knock and wait for them to answer. People want their privacy. I thought that's what the outhouse was for."

Ruth glanced at Blanche and Libby who were biting their lips to keep from laughing. "Thank you, Sheriff. We appreciate you handling this matter."

"You're welcome. I'd like Tadpole to come to the jail a couple of times a week. He and I could talk about things that may be unfamiliar to him that a man wants to ask a man."

"I think that would be a good idea," Blanche said. They all thought Tadpole would benefit from having a role model as good as Sheriff Riverby. Heaven knows the men he'd been with before weren't.

The sheriff left, and Ruth sent Tadpole to the mudroom to wash up. Libby, Blanche, and Ruth fell into each other's arms trying to stifle their laughter.

~~~~~

Massot placed the clamps onto their peg on the wall. He'd finished the last drawer of the dresser and would be moving it out of his shop as soon as he knew the glue was dry. He would varnish it as well as the other pieces where there wasn't so much sawdust.

The light from the open door dimmed, causing him to

look that way. He recognized the silhouette of Kathryn, Ruth's daughter.

"Come on in, honey. What can I do for you?" Massot leaned against the workbench crossing one leg over the other.

"Hi, Mr. Massot. How much would it cost for you to make something for me?" Kathryn came forward, standing awkwardly in front of him.

"Depends on what it is."

"Mama's birthday is coming soon. I want to give her something special."

"What are you thinking of?" Massot looked into her earnest face and knew he would make whatever she wanted. Oh, how he wished she were his daughter. That could never be, of course.

"I was thinking of a nice box for her gloves. The one she has is falling apart. It's not a very good one anyway."

"Would you like to help? We could do it together."

Kathryn's face lit up, then dimmed. "Mama won't want me here that much."

Massot didn't know everything about Ruth's background, but knew enough to understand her reticence on having her daughter be with a man without her supervision. Kathryn was on the cusp of becoming a woman, so he knew she'd become even more cautious. Massot would protect her too, even if she wasn't his daughter. He was going to whether Ruth approved or not.

He thought for a moment. "How about I ask if you can help out down here while she's cleaning my apartment? I can have some things ready for you to work on."

Kathryn looked around. There was sawdust and wood scraps all over that she knew needed to be cleaned up. "That might work."

A smile stretched his lips. He didn't smile often and it felt foreign. "I'll clean up some so there isn't as much to do when you are here. I'll leave enough so it's valid that you're needed."

"Could I pay you in labor for cleaning? I don't have much money."

"That'd be fine." Massot wasn't planning on charging her anything for the glove box. He was simply pleased he could help her make something for her mother. Knowing she had as intimate an article made by him was enough. "Come here. We can pick out the type of wood you want to use. I have several over here."

Soon Kathryn had chosen and was bouncing with excitement as she headed out of his shop. She turned around at the door and said, "I'm so excited. I've never been able to give Mama anything this special before."

"Hold that excitement in, honey, or you'll spoil your surprise."

"Okay." She tried to squash her smile but wasn't too successful. "I'll go pull some weeds. That will help and give me a reason to tell her about why I'm late coming from school."

The door slammed behind her as she flew out. Massot looked out the window and saw her bend over pulling weeds carefully from between the seedlings. Oh, how he wished she was his daughter.

Tadpole came up to her. They talked for a moment then Kathryn showed him how to pick the weeds without hurting the plants. She must have complimented him because he smiled proudly when she said a few more words after he'd pulled some.

Turning back to survey his shop, Massot grabbed the broom and swept up some of the sawdust.

~~~~~

"Mr. Massot is at the door, Miss Ruth. He's asking to speak with you." Tadpole ran into the kitchen where she was fixing lunch. Ruth wiped her hands on a towel and went to find out what he wanted.

"Hello, Mr. Massot. What can I do for you?" Ruth felt a blush creep up her face. She pushed aside the thought that he might have more than a passing interest in her. She didn't want that. Did she? No.

"Good day, ma'am. I'm wondering if it would be possible if your Kathryn would like to earn a little money keeping my shop from getting buried again in sawdust and scraps?"

"Hum, she's in school." Ruth didn't know if letting her be alone with Massot was a good idea.

"I was thinking she could do that while you were cleaning my apartment. That way you'd be close by if she had any questions. I'll be there some, but with spring here now I'll be working more on building the houses I've got contracted."

"You won't be there?" The disappointment Ruth felt surprised her. Even though she cleaned his apartment every Saturday, she didn't see him all that much. He worked in his shop downstairs while she was upstairs. Still, she knew he was there and available for a quick chat or question. Knowing he would not be around while she cleaned disheartened her.

"I'll be there some. Saturdays, I try to get caught up. I may be there when you and she arrive, then head out when I need to."

"I can ask her if she's interested. She's old enough to take on that responsibility. If she is, we'll come at my regular time on Saturday. If she's not, I'll clean your shop for you."

"That sounds like a mighty fine plan, ma'am." Massot tipped his Stetson. "Thank you, I hope to see you both on Saturday."

"Yes, um, good-bye. See you then." Ruth thought it was a rather weak salutation, but couldn't seem to think of something better.

As she walked back to finish making lunch, Tadpole jumped out from behind the dining room door. "You think Kathryn'll want to do the cleaning? If she doesn't, can I? I'd like to earn some money. There's all sorts of things I'd like to buy. There's really keen marbles at the general store. I'd sure like to have my own to play with. The guys are teaching me. I've never had any real toys before. If I earned some money, I could buy my own. You think Mr. Massot might have something I could help him with. I'd like a hoop and stick too. We have to take turns and I can't play with Eddie's when he's in school. He doesn't want it bent or broken."

"Hold on, Tadpole," Ruth said, laughing at the swiftly spewed words. "I have a feeling Kathryn will want to clean Mr. Massot's shop. I can ask him if he needs a short helper. You'd have to work and not play while on the job." She counted out the plates and silverware, handing the flatware to Tadpole. They went into the dining room and began setting the table.

"I can do that. I'm thinking I never had much chance to play before so I know how to work. Always had more chores and work to do just to keep going when I was with the gang. I like it here so much better. Boone and Mae and Nina do too, even though Mae still don't talk. You think she ever will, Miss Ruth?"

"That's something we'll have to pray for, Tadpole. She was hurt really badly by those men. God can heal her, but it may take some time. We need to do all we can to help her feel safe."

"I never knowed about God before I moved here. He seems real helpful. Or at least, if we let Him. Pastor Noah told me that He even sacrificed his Son for me. Just special for me. Well, for everybody else too, but He knowed all that I was going to have happen to me and helped me and the others get left behind so we could be found and come to live here. I were real scared at the time, but I'm real happy that He did that. I love living here with you and the others, but especially you."

Tadpole had finished setting the table and come to Ruth. He wrapped his arms around her, burying his face in her stomach. Tears flooded her eyes and she hugged him close. "I'm real glad He did that too. I'm so happy you all are with us. I love you and the others too." She leaned down and kissed him on the top of his head. "You run upstairs and tell all the others lunch is ready. I'll get it on the table. Be sure to help the twins come down the stairs. We don't want them falling."

"Sure thing, Miss Ruth."

Ruth watched Tadpole run off to do his errand. He was such a sweet precocious boy. He was picking up his lessons well. He normally finished before Mae and Boone. She was pushing the older ones more so they could go to school in the fall without being so far behind.

Nina and the twins played well together and normally stayed upstairs in the corner of the room they used for school after Ruth left to begin lunch. Nina wasn't asking for her mother anymore. Neither were the twins who had lost theirs to the epidemic of measles.

Tadpole had a special place in her heart though. He was always ready to help. He talked a blue streak and was nearly always happy. There had been bumps in adjusting to living in town as well as with so many other children. The House children were used to new people coming to live with them. It was a regular occurrence at Sanctuary Place.

The gang children didn't have any experience with people not of the gang. There had been some battles between the boys that were quickly squelched. Once the rules were explained and boundaries set things had smoothed out.

Footsteps running up the stairs and across the floor above caused Ruth to end her reflections and begin getting lunch served.

CHAPTER SIX

Massot hitched his mules, Milo and Snitch, to his wagon. In it were the last of the furniture he'd built. Climbing into the seat, he took the reins and flicked them, getting the mules to start moving. This was a day he'd been waiting for since he'd been mustered out of the Union Army. The heartbreak he'd suffered when he returned to his hometown had driven him to Stones Creek, Colorado. He'd set up his carpentry shop and begun a successful business. The town was young and needing homes and businesses built. It hadn't taken him long to earn enough to purchase acres far enough out of town so he'd have privacy.

Over the first harsh winter he'd drawn up the plans. The house would be different from any he'd seen or built before. It was a log house, built from logs he'd felled from his land. It didn't look like any other log house or cabin.

It blended into its surroundings, nearly hidden until one was quite close. The first floor had the kitchen, dining room, washroom, entryway, a small sitting room, and a storage room. The stairs wound around the foyer and sitting room that were paneled; the floor, walls and ceiling in boards he'd plained and smoothed to a satiny finish.

There was a pump in the kitchen from the well under the corner of the house. Water could be pumped to the wash room where there were twin laundry sinks. It could also be pumped to the second level.

The second story was larger than the first. A balcony also wrapped around. It was supported on several trees which grew through it, shading the deck as well as the house. Every side of the upper floor was filled with large windows overlooking the forest and the waters of Stones Creek which ran past and on down to run the mill. The creek gave the town its name too. One corner of this floor was a six sided room with a turret that rose to another story. It too had windows on each side.

A great stone fireplace began on the first floor, its chimney in the center and rising to another fireplace on the second floor which provided a warm fire to the master bedroom and the parlor on the other side. The stones Massot had gathered from the creek.

There was also a bathing room with a stove used to heat water for the tub in a large copper tank in the room. The turret also had a stove. Three more bedrooms clustered next to the master bedroom. The parlor ran the length of the floor, overlooking the creek curving around the house. It could be seen from the master bedroom also.

Massot had built the house himself and every piece of furniture. Chairs were made of bent wood, as were the bases of every table. The kitchen cupboards were smoothed wood like on the walls and ceilings of the rooms on the first floor. Shelving was held up by bent wood and wall hooks branched as if growing from the walls themselves.

When the house came into view, Massot pulled the reins, halting the mules. He sat looking at the house he'd built. It was large. Large enough for a family. A family he didn't have. Ruth and Kathryn came to mind. It was almost as if he could see them coming out and waiting for him to get home from work. Another child ran around them toward him. A boy. In his mind's eye, Massot imagined that Ruth was round with his child. He shook his head to clear the vision.

"Git up," Massot said, starting the mules going again. Sitting here dreaming of what couldn't be didn't get this furniture into the house.

As he unloaded the coffee table, he thought about the day before when Kathryn and he began work on the glove box for her mother. She and her mother had come into the shop right after breakfast. Kathryn's eyes sparkled with excitement.

Once Ruth was up in the apartment, Massot had led her over to the work bench and showed her how to sand the boards smooth. He'd done quite a bit the day before so all she had to do was finish it. He carved out the dove tails while she completed her job. Then they set the sides around the bottom, fitting it into the grooves he'd carved. Finally, they glued them in place. That's all they'd do until next week, allowing the glue to dry.

Kathryn then cleaned up all the scraps and swept the sawdust, her payment for the wood and labor to make the box. She also gathered the tools he'd left around the shop and put them in their designated places.

When she was done, Kathryn hugged him, thanking him for his time and help. His chest had constricted with love for the girl. Once again, he wished she were his. In order for that to ever be Massot would have to set the past away. He'd have to be willing to risk being rejected again. He wasn't sure if he could do so.

With the chair and table set in front of the windows overlooking the creek, Massot sat not seeing the beautiful view as he sought direction and courage from his Lord as to his future.

~~~~~

The glove box was finished. It only took three Saturdays to complete. He'd done the preliminary work each week so when Kathryn arrived they could do the steps he'd planned for that day.

One thing he'd done, without discussing it with her, was carve a large heart with two small ones interlocking with it on the top. When Kathryn had seen it she'd squealed and hugged him, jumping back when Ruth came down to see what the noise was for. He'd covered the box with a rag while Kathryn claimed a mouse had scared her. Once Ruth was back in the apartment, they had laughed holding their hands over their mouths to keep her from hearing. Massot had cautioned her about fibbing.

It was Thursday, after lunch. Massot knew Blanche would be home now after working in the cafe she owned with Almeda Wilson and Chloe McIlroy. The twins and Nina would be napping. He hoped Ruth would have time for a walk with him.

With his hat in his hand, Massot knocked on the front door of Sanctuary House. He'd prayed that Ruth would answer and sent up a quick thank you when she did.

"Afternoon, Mr. Massot. What brings you to the

House?" Ruth smiled at him and his insides flipped just a bit.

"I was hoping you had some time to take a walk with me. It concerns your cleaning for me. I'd like to discuss something with you."

"Oh, um, I suppose so. I'll need to let Blanche know I'm leaving for a while. Just a moment."

"Thank you ma'am. I'll wait out here on the porch." He stepped back and Ruth closed the door.

When she appeared she had on her hat and gloves, with a shawl wrapped around her shoulders. She blushed as she passed him then preceded him down the steps. When they reached the street, she said, "Where did you want to walk?"

"It's a few minutes outside of town, this way." Massot pointed into the woods behind his shop.

"Oh." Ruth hesitated, obviously uneasy.

"Don't worry. I just want to show you something. I want to know if you want to continue cleaning for me."

"And we need to walk in the woods for that?" Ruth gave him a sideways look.

"Well, yes. I've built a house and moved in. I'm hoping you'll want to keep cleaning for me, but it's in the woods a little ways from town. I'll understand if you don't want to."

"You built a house? You never told me you were doing so."

"I've been working on it for several years. Did it all myself. The furnishings, too. It's, um, not your typical house. I'd like you to see it." Massot stuck his hands in his pockets to keep from taking hers.

"I'd love to see it. Which way?" They'd entered the forest and were walking side by side.

"It's about a five or ten minute walk."

The forest of aspen and pine enclosed them, the silvery leaves quaking in the breeze. The air was fresh and cool in the dimness of the tall trees. They walked in silence for a while then she asked, "Does anyone know you have a house out here?"

"Not many. Ben Cutler knows and the sheriff. I've a feeling Pastor Noah does. He seems to know just about everything that goes on around here."

"Yes, he does. Or at least he pretends to. He's been a real help with Boone and Tadpole. He's teaching all of them, well the three older children, several times a week about faith and Jesus. They hadn't ever heard anything other than His name as a curse word. Other inappropriate words also seem to be well known. He's been able to explain why they aren't used in polite society."

Massot chuckled. "I'm sure Tadpole wanted to know why more than Boone did."

Ruth laughed. "Yes, and he made sure to tell me which words Pastor Noah told them not to use in explicit detail on each word."

"Saying them, of course."

"Of course."

The house came into view and Ruth gasped. "Oh, Massot. It's beautiful. How did you do this all by yourself?"

"Time, strength and patience. It was a lot of work over several years. It's done now and I've moved in. Come, let me show you."

They entered and Ruth dropped her mouth open. Massot showed her the downstairs, explaining the various features he'd built in. When they went upstairs,

Ruth was drawn to the windows overlooking the creek. Massot opened the door to the balcony. They went out and up to the railing.

"Oh my, what a beautiful view. You picked a wonderful spot for your house."

"I like it. I'm above the high water so there's no worry about it flooding. The balcony wraps around by the master bedroom also. There will be chairs and a table or two out here next summer. Those are winter projects." Massot opened the door so she could enter.

"What a beautiful fireplace. The stones are from the creek aren't they?" Ruth drew close examining the stones and ran her hand across the wooden beam mantel.

"From farther up the hillside. There's another firebox in the master. Come, I'll show you the rest of the place."

He led the way, showing her the three smaller bedrooms, the bathing room, and finally the master bedroom. The view of the forest from the windows was spectacular from each room, but the one in the master was another view of the creek.

"You did a wonderful job building this. That turret room is lovely. What do you plan to use it for?"

"An office. The upper room hasn't been finished yet. No need as I'm the only one living here." Massot eyed Ruth trying to determine if she might be interested in living here. She walked around the room gently touching each piece of furniture. She'd done the same in each room they went in.

"Would you be interested in keeping this place clean? I doubt I'd track as much sawdust in after the walk from my shop."

"Truthfully, I'll have to think about it. Being this far from town and the home of a bachelor..." She let the sentence drop. "Even being here with you now is questionable for my reputation. Especially standing in this room."

"You've seen the entire house so let's head back to town. You can think about it and let me know."

~~~~~

"So, what did Mr. Massot want to speak with you about?" Blanche sat beside Ruth on the wide front porch as the children played in the yard. It was Laura's and Libby's day to fix supper so neither woman had any chores to do at the moment. Ruth was darning a sock and Blanche was mending a tear in one of her sons' trousers.

"Did you know he's built a house in the woods?" Ruth laid her hands in her lap. "It's about a five or ten minute walk." She pointed in the general direction of the house.

"No, what's it like?"

"Like nothing you've ever seen before. Made from logs but the second story is larger than the first." Ruth went on to explain the details of the house and Massot's request that she keep cleaning for him. On the walk back to town he'd asked if she would help him by sewing drapes and curtains. Help pick out the fabrics and trims. The lack of any type of softening of the decor left the house looking bare and unlived in.

"Are you going to? It's far out and you'll be alone with a man. That's not going to keep the gossips from having a hay day."

"I know." Ruth sat silently gazing out over the yard. Tadpole and Mark Duffle were wrestling. Though older, Tadpole was smaller. When Mark tossed him to the ground Tadpole jumped up and hit Mark in the stomach. Ruth started to get up, but Blanche laid a hand on her arm.

"Oof." Mark let out a pained breath.

"Wait. Let's see how they handle this," Blanche said.

"Wow, good punch," Mark said with a smile.

"Yeah, you took me down good too." Tadpole wrapped his arm around Mark and the two ran over to where some of the other boys were whittling. They were too young yet, so they didn't have the knives the older boys had.

"See, they worked it out. Boys are very different than girls." Blanche picked up her mending.

"You'd think I would know that. I've lived with so many boys ever since I came to Sanctuary Place and now here at the House."

"It's different when they are yours."

The sound of a horse approaching had both ladies looking up the street. Hawk Conner came into view. Hawk was the owner of Hawk's Wing Ranch. He'd gone with the posse that found the children and gained Mae's trust when she rode in front of him as they came to town.

Mae didn't trust easily. The ten-year-old had been abused by the men of the King gang and no longer spoke. All the ladies hoped the love and security in Sanctuary House would help her heal from her trauma.

Hawk swung down from the saddle and wrapped the reins around the hitching post. "Howdy, ladies." He tipped his hat to them as the children swarmed around all talking at once.

Mae squeezed through the group and hugged Hawk

who returned it. She smiled up at him.

"How you doing, pipsqueak?"

She smiled and nodded.

Hawk glanced up at Ruth and Blanche who shook her head slightly. He ruffled Mae's hair. "You doing your lessons well?"

She nodded again.

Hawk looked over the other children. "How about the rest of you? You all studying hard?" A chorus of affirmative answers rang out. Hawk pulled a paper bag from the pocket of his black duster coat. "Here Mae, pass these out. Since everyone is working so hard, everyone gets a peppermint stick."

Mae grinned as she took the bag and began handing out the treats. Hawk extricated himself from the pack and strode to the porch, putting his foot on the highest step, leaning his elbow on his knee.

"Afternoon, Mrs. Basking, Miss Naylor. Mighty fine day. Thought I'd stop by and see after the four new additions to the House."

Ruth saw a tinge of pink on Blanche's cheeks. "They seem to be adjusting well. There have been a few pitfalls but nothing truly major."

Tadpole ran up just then. "Did ja hear I saw Mrs. Fugard in her altogether? She's real skinny under all those clothes." Red from the peppermint stick he held in his hand was smeared across his cheeks.

"Tadpole, you were instructed by several people, including the sheriff and Pastor Noah not to mention that incident. It's very upsetting to Mrs. Fugard. Now go on with you and let us talk. You aren't to interrupt," Ruth scolded.

Hawk leaned down and loudly whispered, "I heard.

It's not polite to talk about a lady like that."

"She ain't no lady. She can screech like a hoot owl."

"Tadpole!" Ruth's sharp voice made Tadpole run back to the children after flashing a quick grin at Hawk.

Ruth just shook her head. That boy was definitely precocious.

"How's Mae doing? Has she spoken yet?" Since his question seemed to be addressed to Blanche, Ruth stayed silent.

"Not yet, but we have hope. She's becoming more relaxed and doesn't startle at every little sound." Blanche looked up.

"Glad to hear it. How're Boone and Nina doing? Tadpole seems to be acting like a regular boy his age, getting into trouble and talking all the time."

Ruth and Blanche chuckled. "That he is," Ruth said. "He's a dear child. Seems to remember everything and tells it all. Even things he shouldn't."

"Boone and Mae hope to be ready to go to school come fall. Boone's very protective of the others and is beginning to extend that to the House children. Soon we won't be differentiating between them. They will just all be children of the House."

They chatted for a few more minutes, then Hawk tipped his hat again and went over to speak once more to the children, then mounted. He waved as he set the horse to a canter.

"Blanche, I think he's sweet on you," Ruth said with a grin.

Her friend blushed again. "No more so than Massot is sweet on you."

Ruth was dumbstruck. Massot was sweet on her?

No, that couldn't be. The tightening in Ruth's stomach confused her. Was it caused by attraction or fear?

CHAPTER SEVEN

The back door slammed and Libby Trembly stomped from the wash room into the kitchen. Arleta ran to her, holding her arms out to be picked up. She'd been fussy ever since she woke from her nap and found that Libby was gone.

"What's got you all riled up?" Ruth was ironing sheets on the kitchen work table.

Libby pulled out a chair and sat down, Arleta on her lap. "It's that new lawyer, Forsyth Franklin Fredrick Farnsworth the fourth, pretentious twit. I went to see if he'd handle me adopting the twins. You know what he said, the greenhorn?"

"What?"

"He told me I couldn't adopt them because I'm not married. Said he'd help me find a couple who would take them. He knows several back cast. Arrogant mush-head." Tears slid down Libby's face.

"Oh, honey, no. Surely not." Ruth set the sad-iron back on the stove and came around giving Libby a hug.

"That's what he said. Said I couldn't possibly raise them without a husband. What does he think all the ladies of Sanctuary House do? You all are raising your children just fine. Sure you want husbands. That's why you all came out here. I understand that. I'm not ready to marry yet. I'm still mourning Tim and my sons. I don't want to marry any old man just so I can adopt the twins. Lucy gave them to me before she passed. They are mine." Libby was crying now.

"Pastor Noah knows that. He heard Lucy when she gave them to you. I heard too, but I'm not sure if my word would sway Mr. Farnsworth." Ruth patted Libby on the back.

"Well, I can't deal with it right now. I've got to go change this little one. She stinks." Libby kissed Arleta on the top of her head and stood. She wiped the tears from her cheeks. "Where's Jack?"

"He and Nina are playing in the parlor with Boone and Mae watching them. With the rain of the past few days I didn't want them outside getting all muddy. Boone wasn't happy about it, but he did mind."

"Is Jack still following Tadpole around?"

"Most of the time. I sent Tadpole upstairs before Jack woke from his nap. He needs to spend some more time on his letters. Hopefully, he's doing so. I have been ironing the sheets and haven't gone up to check."

Libby left with Arleta, leaving Ruth to her ironing. She glanced at the clock. School would let out soon. She needed to get snacks ready. It was a time of the day that Ruth enjoyed. All the children gathered around the tables and shared their day. She had the ones who went to school speak first, then the others. Everyone seemed to enjoy the time before going to play, do chores, or homework.

The front door opened with boys and girls flooding in chattering amongst themselves and with the others who spent the day at the House. Ruth noticed a few extras. They weren't really extras. They were children who used to live at the House but whose mothers had married local men and now lived elsewhere. Eddie and Mark Duffle would be moving across the alley into an apartment above the barber and bath shop when their mother Laura married Hank Johnson in June.

Dunc and Lil Pen were there. Chloe had asked that they spend the afternoon at the house. Both ladies were hoping Dunc would be a good influence on Boone. They were near the same age, and Dunc had known the boy before Chloe and he were abandoned. Lil Pen wasn't in school yet as she was only five. There was no way she was going to be left behind if her big brother was going to come to the House.

Ruth was busy pouring milk and limiting the cookies each child consumed. Once that was done she sat at the end of the table surveying and listening. Tadpole had come downstairs and was stuffing his mouth full of snickerdoodles.

Until he and the others were rescued they'd never had cookies before. Desserts of any kind weren't something they were familiar with. It broke Ruth's heart to know the deprivation the four young souls had gone through their entire lives. She was doing all she could to give them love, acceptance, and allowing them an extra dessert if they ate their lunches well. That was the only meal she had final say over. She figured a little spoiling wouldn't hurt.

Ruth noticed that Kathryn wasn't her normal happy self. She was sitting quietly eating her snack. Her posture was perfect and her shoulders seemed to be stiff. Something was bothering her. Ruth would question her later when they were alone.

~~~~~

It wasn't until much later that Ruth was able to find out what was concerning Kathryn. Once the snacks were consumed and the tales of the day told, the children had scattered. Some went to do their chores, some played. Others had homework. Kathryn claimed to have homework but didn't have any books with her. Now it was bedtime, the perfect time to find out as Ruth brushed her daughter's hair.

"Kathryn, honey, is something bothering you? I noticed you haven't been your normal happy, friendly self tonight. You didn't want to read to Nina. She was very disappointed.

"I know. I'm sorry. I just don't feel like it." Kathryn didn't make eye contact with Ruth in the mirror as she sat before her. Silence met her. That was not like her daughter. She normally shared everything with Ruth, except for birthday or Christmas gifts. She placed her hands on Kathryn's shoulders and turned her on the low stool.

"What is it, honey?" Ruth studied her daughter's solemn face.

"You know how you tell me to be aware and notice things. To trust my feelings." She swallowed. "I have a feeling like I'm being watched."

The bottom of Ruth's stomach fell out. *No, Lord, please.* What was she going to do? How could she let Kathryn out of her sight? She couldn't keep her home from school. Couldn't restrict her to her room. Couldn't wrap her in cotton wool. But she couldn't let what happened to her happen to Kathryn.

Ruth stroked Kathryn's face. "Thank you for telling me. Believe your feeling. You know what I went through. That's why I've warned you to be watchful and listen to your instincts. We'll work out a plan."

"I want to go to school. I want to play and visit with my friends. I don't want to be afraid and hide." Kathryn's eyes were wide with worry.

"Rest easy. The best you can do is stay alert. Stay with other children, especially those from the House. Be sure to tell me where you are going and with who.

"I'm going to talk with the other Ladies. We'll make sure we all watch too. If there is someone, and I believe you are right, with all of us watching we'll figure out who. He'll make a mistake. Then we'll know and we can stop him."

Ruth hugged Kathryn to her. As they clung to each other, drawing what comfort and security they could, Ruth began to pray.

"Father in heaven, You know our thoughts and our fears. You know all that goes on. You know our worry. We thank You for Your protection, that You have gathered us under Your wings as the hen gathers her chicks. We ask that You give us peace in the knowledge that You are there. That we have nothing to fear because fear is not of You. We choose to believe Your promises. We choose to have faith in Your Word. Thank you, Lord, that because we have Your Son, in whose name we pray, we can come to Your throne confident that we will receive grace and mercy. Help us now to make the right choices and decisions. Amen."

Kathryn's amen was softer but her body relaxed against Ruth's. A huge yawn made Ruth smile. Peace was descending on both of them. They would sleep without worry because they were tucked close to the One in control, protected under His wings.

~~~~~

Ruth pressed her hand to her stomach as she descended the stairs. The Ladies were in the parlor for some adult time after the children were down for the night. As much as she wanted to ignore Kathryn's feelings, there was no way she was going to. The Ladies needed to know so they could watch too.

She sat down in a chair and looked around the room. Blanche Basking, the oldest of them, was the unofficial leader. Laura Duffle would be marrying sometime in June to Hank Johnson. Libby Trembly had come with Gema Volkovichna in January.

Libby had lost her husband, three-year-old son and six-month-old son when the riverboat they'd been on exploded. Ending up at Sanctuary Place in deep depression, the matron thought leaving the river where she'd lost so much would help Libby. Coming had brought more loss but also gain in that the death of Lucy Tanner had brought her the twins to raise.

Of the eight ladies who had come to Stones Creek last summer, only three were left. The others were married and most still lived in town.

"I've got a problem I want to discuss with you," Ruth began. The chatter stopped and everyone looked at her. Taking a deep breath, she said, "Kathryn feels like she's being watched. She told me so tonight."

Expressions of concern filled the next moments. The Ladies knew Ruth's past. They knew she was leery of men in general. They all were vigilant in concern for their children and themselves. They'd stepped up their attentiveness after Gema's kidnapping by the King

Gang. It was the same gang who abandoned the children.

"I'm so scared. If anything happened to Kathryn I don't know what I'd do."

Blanche leaned over and patted Ruth's knee. "We'll keep watch and make sure nothing happens to her. Also, we need to let Sheriff Riverby know. That way he can be on the lookout too."

"Do you think it's the King Gang? They took Chloe when she was younger than Kathryn. Look what they did to Mae." Ruth tried to stem the shaking of her hands. The paling of the other ladies' faces showed they were concerned about that same thing.

~~~~~

Massot watched Ruth as she and the children worked in the garden. Tadpole was talking, as usual, weeding the row next to hers. Mae and Boone knelt around the tomato plants they'd recently put in. Nina, Jack, and Arleta played in the dirt, faces covered with brown smudges.

Something wasn't quite right. Ruth's stance and movements seemed stiff and anxious. Often she looked up from her hoeing and around as if searching for something. Or someone. He scanned the street and what he could see from his window.

If there was someone spying on the House occupants, Massot was going to know it. He left the shop and went around the building to the garden. Nina looked up at him and grinned. The twins turned to look and smiled. Their white teeth weren't white anymore.

Ruth looked up from her hoeing and spied the dirty little ones. "Oh, don't eat the dirt. If you want to be with us you have to be good." She hurried over and pulled a rag from the pocket of her apron. Massot was impressed that all three children allowed her to wipe dirt from cheeks and mouths.

"It must be a challenge to get the weeding done as well as mind the children."

"It can be a chore. I want to make sure we have a handle on the weeds and the older ones know what's a weed and what's a vegetable so I can set them loose here by themselves. It's a good responsibility for them. When school's out, the others will help too." Ruth wiped her hands on her rag, not getting all the soil off.

Massot took her by the elbow and led her to the wall of his shop. "Is everything all right?"

Startled eyes met his. "Wh… Why do you ask?"

"I was watching from the window and noticed you were looking around as if searching for someone."

Ruth rubbed her face with her hands. Dirt smeared across her cheeks. Massot placed his hand on hers. "Stop, you'll get dirt in your eyes." Her face was soft, even with the smudges. He wanted to stroke her skin, drinking in the smoothness. He pulled his hand away.

Ruth gazed off into the forest. He could tell she wasn't seeing the trees. There was something in her eyes that spoke of pain buried deep.

She let out a long sigh and turned back to him. "I'm worried. Kathryn told me she feels like she's being watched. Not the way you watched us out the window. The feelings she has is of evil intent. It makes her nervous and scared. I'm afraid someone will do something to her. Some man." The last words were nearly whispered.

"When did she tell you this?" Massots hands

clenched into fists. His voice more gravelly than usual. He wanted to punch something, or someone. Kathryn should never be afraid.

"A couple of days ago. I told the other Ladies and the older boys. They can help watch out for her while they are at school. These," she waved to those in the garden, "don't know. We don't want to scare them."

"Do you have any idea who it might be?"

She looked away again, then back at him. "Not for sure. There are just so many men here in the West." A shaky hand tucked a lock of hair behind her ear.

"So you suspect someone? Who?" Massot clenched his fist. No one was going to hurt Kathryn if he could do anything to prevent it.

"I don't want to say anything since I don't have any real proof."

"I can understand that, but if I'm going to watch out for her, it would help to know."

"You want to help watch?"

Her surprise at the firmness of his words dismayed him. Why wouldn't he want to help? Massot took her hand and gave it a gentle squeeze. "Of course I want to help. She's a wonderful girl. You've done so well raising her. I don't want anything to happen to any of the people of the House, especially Kathryn. I suppose it's because I know you and her so much better than the others." He trailed off.

Tadpole bounced up then. "You coming to the birthday party? It's next Sunday after church. All the Ladies are coming, even those what got married and all their children. It should be a grand time."

Massot leaned down. "Oh? Whose birthday is it? Yours?"

"Nah, I ain't got a birthday." Tadpole screwed his mouth to the side. "How'd I get born if I ain't got a birthday?"

Ruth stroked his hair. "You have a birthday. It's just that we don't know when it is. I suppose you can pick a day to be your birthday."

Tadpole screwed his mouth to the other side. "That's a powerful important thing, choosing a birthday. Not many people get to do that. I suppose Mae and Nina and Boone ain't got birthdays either. I'm gonna have to do some powerful thinking to choose my day." He turned and ran back to the others, no doubt to tell them they had to choose a birthday.

Massot looked at Ruth. They both laughed. "It's a powerful important decision. I'm pretty sure it will take some days to choose."

Ruth looked up at him. "Would you like to come to the party?"

"I might. Whose is it?" He knew, of course, but didn't want to give Kathryn's secret away.

Ruth cleared her throat. "Mine."

"I'd be delighted, ma'am. Thank you for the invite."

Ruth blushed and told him of the time, then turned and crossed the garden. Jack had muddy lips. Massot watched her gently wipe the grime from his mouth.

He wanted her. Wanted her as a husband wants his wife. Wanted Kathryn as his daughter. Wanted to see Ruth round with his child. He went back into his shop wondering if he was enough for her. She didn't seem to want a lot. Maybe it was time to see what he had to offer.

CHAPTER EIGHT

Massot stepped into the bank and waited near the door while CJ Ritter finished helping another person. He'd been brought to Stones Creek as president of the bank Nugget Nate Ryder had started two years ago. He was married and Massot had heard the man's wife was expecting.

"So long," CJ said as the cowboy left. "Howdy, Massot. Don't see you here that often. Have another deposit to make?" The banker was grinning from ear to ear. Much wider than any time Massot had come in the past.

"You seem pretty jovial today."

"I am. Yes, sir, I sure am. My wife had the baby yesterday. A little girl. Named her Erma after my grandmother. Both are doing fine."

"Congratulations." Massot shook his hand, thinking that maybe, just maybe that would be him someday announcing the birth of his child.

"So, do you have a deposit?"

"Not today. I'd like to see what my balance is. My bank book isn't up to date."

CJ frowned at him. "I know. You never bring it with

73

you when you come in. Let me get it."

When he came back with the bank's copy, CJ opened it and set it on the counter facing Massot.

His eyes widened as he looked at the balance. "This can't be right. That's got to be too much."

"It's right. I've got the receipts for each of your deposits."

"But…" Massot didn't know what to say. How could he have so much money in his account? He looked over the columns. Dates of deposits and the amounts he'd added to his account. Looking up, he said, "I can't believe it."

CJ grinned. "Look here. See this column? It says 'Debits.' You see any entries in that column?" He flipped the pages slowly back to the beginning of the book. There weren't many numbers in the debit column.

Massot shook his head, trying to settle the whirling in it. He was wealthy. Not like the railroad barons or Nugget Nate, but he had a large nest egg. With his working as steadily as he did, he would be able to support a wife and family.

"Huh." He lifted one side of his mouth in a lopsided grin. The memory of a woman telling him she wouldn't marry a man who only wanted to be a carpenter. That he'd not be able to give her the things she wanted if he didn't aspire to loftier goals. Seems she was wrong. He could give her more than she'd ever imagined. Her image faded and Ruth's quiet, calm smile replaced it.

"Thanks CJ. That's all I wanted, to know the balance. I'll be finishing Eli's house in a couple of weeks and bring in a deposit then.

"Tell Mrs. Ritter, I'm glad she came through her

confinement well and I'll be pleased to make over the baby when I see them."

CJ pulled the bank book back and closed it. "Will do. You have a good day now."

"I will. Thanks."

~~~~~

Massot worked up the courage to request a meeting with the committee of men responsible for screening anyone wanting to court any of the House Ladies. It was a safeguard Nugget Nate had set up so the women could be assured the men who were interested in the possibility of marrying any of them were upstanding, honest, hardworking men who would treat the women and children well.

On Thursday, Massot went to Pastor Noah's gun shop and requested to meet with the committee. Noah smiled and said he'd set it up for the next day. Massot was surprised he didn't ask who he intended to court. Then he realized there were only three women left in the house. It could be any one of them. He was thirty-eight. The ladies ranged from Blanche Basking at thirty-five, Ruth, who would be thirty on Sunday, and Libby, who he thought was in her mid-twenties.

He'd dressed carefully, making sure he put on a clean shirt, one without any holes or buttons missing. When he got to the shop he stopped and combed his hair. He didn't want it sticking up when he took his hat off in the general store. Massot was meeting Noah at the gun shop, then they'd cross over to gather in the back room of the store. Sheriff Riverby and Eli Steele rounded out the four men on the committee.

Butterflies battled for escape in his belly. When he arrived at the gun shop, Noah exited. He was dressed as usual in severe black, broken only by the white of his shirt. Massot rubbed his sweaty palms on his trouser legs.

Noah must have seen that he was nervous. He slapped Massot on the back. "You're not going to your execution. Relax." Then he chuckled. "Well, maybe you are. Some men think marriage is a death sentence."

As they climbed the boardwalk steps at the corner of the dress shop, Sheriff Riverby and Eli crossed from the doctor's office. Massot saw smiles of greeting and the butterflies subsided some.

Ben waved them back from behind the counter. In the back room was a table with chairs and five mugs set out. The aroma of fresh coffee lent a welcoming air to the place.

Once they were all seated with filled mugs, Noah began. "You've been here all the time we've had the Ladies in town. You know the requirements. We know you and your character. All we need to know is which Lady you are interested in courting."

"That's all you need?" Massot wondered if they would reject his request if he chose the wrong Lady. "I'm wanting to court Ruth Naylor. She's been cleaning for me and we've gotten acquainted during those times. She's also planted a garden for the House beside my shop. She and the children work in it and we chat some."

"What are your thoughts about Kathryn?" Ben asked.

Massot smiled. "She's a sweetheart. I'm hoping she allows me to adopt her. Don't tell, but she asked me to make a glove box for her mother for her birthday this Sunday. We made it together. She's mighty proud of it."

He couldn't seem to keep his pride in her from his voice.

"She must trust you to ask for your help," Eli said. The men were all smiling.

"Well, I suppose so. I think I'm a pretty trustworthy man."

"We do too, Massot." Sheriff Riverby took a swallow of coffee.

"Massot," Noah said. "We'd be pleased to have you court Ruth Naylor. Be aware she's been deeply hurt in the past. Court her carefully."

"Thank you, I will." Massot couldn't believe that was all it took. He'd thought there'd be a raft of questions and rules he had to follow. "Um, that's all? No questions or orders?"

"Massot, we know you," Noah said. "We, as a committee, listed the men we knew would be approved as soon as we met the first time. You were one on that list. You fit what Nate wants for all the Ladies. You could have said any of the names and we would approve you."

"You mean I put on my second-best shirt and took a bath last night and didn't need to?" Massot never imagined it would be so easy to get approval.

All four men laughed at him.

"No, you didn't." Ben slapped him on the back. "But thanks anyway. Especially for taking a bath."

CHAPTER NINE

Tadpole dragged Ruth by the hand away from the church. He wanted to get the birthday party started. He'd never been to one. Never seen any kind of celebration for someone. The only celebrating he'd seen was after a successful heist. The men of the King Gang would get drunk and make the women cry. The children stayed away, hidden by their mothers or others.

"Tadpole," Ruth laughed. "We have to get lunch ready and eat before we have the party."

"I know, but everybody will be here for lunch. The faster we get there, the sooner we can eat, and the sooner the party'll start."

Ruth looked back at a smiling Kathryn trailing behind, and let him drag her to the house. "Normal Sunday routine, Tadpole. Change, then I think you are on table setting duty. Don't shirk your chore."

"Yes, ma'am." He ran up the stairs and she could hear his thundering steps across the floor through the ceiling. Ruth shook her head and headed to the kitchen. Even though it was her birthday, she had duties there.

It wasn't long before the others began coming into the house. The day was warm and sunny for mid-April. Warmer than usual. It would mean the children could go outside to play and the adults could visit in the dining room after eating. They wouldn't even need jackets.

Ruth brought a large bowl of mashed potatoes into the dining room. The room was filling with parents and children. Massot was holding on to Kathryn's hand. She was smiling up at him. They went to the small table and Kathryn pointed to a brown paper wrapped package. She smiled up at Massot who returned it.

Soon everyone was seated, and Blanche gave the blessing mentioning Ruth especially. Kathryn had Massot sitting next to her, across from Ruth who was next to Tadpole. The boy talked excitedly about birthdays and his problem of deciding when his would be.

Once lunch was over, before they served the birthday cake, the gifts were brought to Ruth. Kathryn's smile was so wide Ruth thought her lips might split. Tadpole bounced on the chair next to her.

The Ladies gave her a new apron, a scented soap, and a pair of silk stockings, which she covered back up as her cheeks got red. Kathryn pushed her package across the table.

"Massot and I made this for you, Mama."

Ruth looked at her daughter then at the carpenter. "Thank you." Untying the string, she pulled the paper off. "Oh, my. This is lovely, Kathryn. You did this?"

She touched the interlaced hearts on the top, then opened the top. There was a brass latch to keep the box closed. It was smooth both on the inside and out. She ran her finger over the swirling grain of the wood.

"Massot helped, but it was my idea."

Kathryn came around the table and hugged her mother. "I wanted something special for you. I love you. I wanted to let you know how much."

Tears flooded Ruth's eyes as she held her daughter to her. "I love you too." She glanced at Massot and saw something in his eyes that made her insides curl. She could barely pull her eyes away.

"Let me see." Tadpole got on his knees and closed then opened the box. "Wow, Kathryn. That's really something. Mr. Massot, can I make something too?"

The cake being served took the boy's attention allowing Massot not to answer. Ruth would have to explain that it wasn't always polite to ask someone for a favor in public.

Chocolate stained many faces and had to be washed before the children were allowed to go play outside. Ozzy, Dunc, and Kathryn were charged with watching that the little ones didn't wander. The twins and Nina (who protested), and several of the married Ladies' youngest were put down for naps.

Since it was Ruth's birthday she was excused from her washing dishes duty. She and the other adults moved to other tables to allow for easier conversation. Massot sat next to her.

"Thank you for helping Kathryn. You didn't need to do that."

"She traded cleaning my shop for the wood and labor. I enjoyed working with her. She's a good worker." Massot leaned down and whispered, "Any progress on who might be watching her?"

"No, I'm hoping she tells me she doesn't think she's

still having that feeling."

The couples and Ladies laughed and chatted over coffee. Having most of the Ladies who had lived in the House together was special. Ruth loved them all and since the marriages she didn't see them as often.

The front door slammed and Mae ran in, going straight to Blanche. She grabbed her hand and pulled.

"What it is, sweetie?"

Mae just pulled and pointed to the door. All the adults stood to head out. A yell, screams, and a splash followed by a yowl had them all running.

~~~~~

Ruth followed several of the men who got to the door first. Kathryn was just coming up the steps.

"I told him not to. He wouldn't listen." Tears were streaming down her face. She pointed to the corner of the porch.

Ozzie and Boone were holding Tadpole who was dripping wet hanging half out of the rain barrel.

"He climbed up onto the roof and jumped off. I think he's hurt," Ozzie yelled. The teens were not able to lift him up enough to get him out of the barrel.

Ruth's heart beat hard in her chest as she watched McIlroy and Massot haul the crying boy out and lay him on the ground. She ran to the edge of the porch and looked down at him.

Doc Eli knelt beside him. He lifted Tadpole's left arm which was bent between the wrist and elbow. Ruth pressed one hand to her mouth, the other to her chest. The arm looked broken to her.

"It's broken. I'll need to take him to the clinic to set and put a cast on." Eli laid the arm across Tadpole's chest. "Don't move that if you can hold it still. I'm going to carry you." He picked up the boy gently and strode up the street. Ruth hurried to follow.

"I told him not to jump. I told him, but he wouldn't listen." Kathryn was weeping.

"It's going to be okay. Doc will fix him up. You stay with Libby and Blanche. I'm going to be with him. He'll be scared." Ruth hugged her daughter and handed her to Blanche.

Massot joined her on the walk to the clinic. "That boy is a pistol, that's for sure. Jumping off the roof into a rain barrel." He shook his head as they hurried across the street.

"Why would he do something like that?" Ruth wiped the tears from her cheeks.

Massot chuckled. "That's boys. I did some pretty lame-brained stunts when I was a boy."

They entered the clinic and went straight to the exam room where Doc Eli was removing the clothing from the soaking wet boy. Tadpole had stopped crying, but pain was written all over his face.

"I'm going to cut this shirt off. I don't want to try to get it off over the break." Eli cut along the seam up the side and along the seam of the sleeve. "Maybe you can sew it back together."

Ruth took the shirt and other items as they were removed. "I should have thought to get dry clothing and bring it."

Eli wrapped Tadpole in a sheet with only his left arm out. "Massot, I want you to hold him. I'm going to set the arm."

When Eli pulled the arm, Tadpole let out a scream and began crying again. Eli laid the arm down in

Tadpole's lap and signaled to Ruth to approach, and started to gather what he needed to apply the cast.

She came and wrapped her arms around him carefully so as not to jostle the arm. "The worst is over, Tadpole." She kissed his head. "Doc will put a cast on it to hold it in place until the bones heal." Tadpole just cried on her shoulder.

Eli wrapped the arm in strips of muslin, then slathered plaster all over the arm he'd bent at a right angle.

Blanche came in with dry clothing. "Is he going to be all right?" Her worry was evident in her tone.

"Yes. It was a clean break. We got it set easily," Eli said.

"Easily?" Tadpole hollered. "It hurt like…" Massot covered his mouth before the last word came out. The adults exchanged amused glances. They all knew a swear word was going to end the sentence.

"I know it did, Tadpole." Eli brushed a speck of plaster on his nose. "I meant that it went back together as it should without any problem." Finished with the cast, he began washing up.

Massot was behind Tadpole, holding the arm up off the table so Eli could plaster it. "How long before this dries so he can go home?"

"Half hour to forty-five minutes. Then I want him in bed for the rest of the day." Eli gave Tadpole a severe look. "No jumping off roofs."

Ruth leaned over and looked in Tadpole's tear-streaked face. "Why did you jump off the roof?"

"We always jumped into a lake or stream or such on the first really warm day. The water was cold but it was so much fun. There's no water except the rain barrel.

Seemed good enough."

"Was it?" Ruth raised her eyebrows at him.

"Not so much. It was until my arm smacked the barrel. Then it wasn't."

Blanche stroked Tadpole's head. "You'll be sore for a while and that cast will be on for a long time. Long enough for you to think about things you should have thought about before you jumped.

"I'm glad you weren't hurt more. I'm going back to the House and letting Mae know you are going to be fine. She's very upset. You might want to tell her you are sorry you scared her so badly."

Tadpole nodded and leaned against Ruth. He yawned. The injury, emotions, and setting the arm exhausted him. She wrapped her arm around him and kissed his hair again.

"Not much longer, Tadpole. Then we'll take you home and you can rest up."

"I don't want to go to bed. I want to show everyone my cast."

"They can see it as we go into the House or at supper. Doc Eli told you to go to bed for the rest of the day. We will follow doctor's orders."

"Okay." Tadpole yawned again.

Ruth looked at Massot as he stroked the boy's hair.

CHAPTER TEN

Massot watched Ruth approach his house. She'd decided to continue cleaning for him. Normally he was away by the time she got there. He had houses to complete and start. Not having any workers hired put all the load on him. He didn't mind. He enjoyed being by himself.

As soon as he spoke to her, Massot would head to town. He was finishing up the house he was building for Eli and Leah Steele. Then he'd start on the house he was building for Chloe and McIlroy. After that was one for the new lawyer, Forsyth Franklin Fredrick Farnsworth the Fourth, who was being called Four in town.

Massot ran a hand over his hair, hoping none of it stuck up. He wanted to look as sharp as he could in his work clothes. This was the day he was going to ask to court Ruth.

The morning was sunny, the creek glistened, throwing sparkles as the water tumbled over the stones. No breeze ruffled the leaves. Birds sang and fluttered throughout the trees. Everything smelled fresh and clean. The day was beautiful though Massot thought the woman walking toward him more beautiful than nature could possibly be.

He stepped out from the shadows created by the second story of his house and walked toward Ruth. She looked at him and waved, smiling.

"I thought you'd be banging a hammer on Doc and Leah's house." Ruth tipped the brim of her bonnet back so she could see him better as they stood on the pine needle covered ground.

"I wanted to wait and speak with you. Will you walk with me to the creek? It's lovely this morning." They turned and went past the entrance and around, walking down the gentle slope to the edge of the creek.

Ruth stood on the bank, looking across at a broad plain extending to the tree line. A few elk grazed in the meadow. A hawk soared overhead. "This is a wonderful view. Every time I clean I look out the window and see wildlife there or coming to drink."

Massot came to stand beside her. He reached out slowly and took her hand. "Ruth, how would you like to see this view every day?" Her hand started trembling in his. He hoped it was because she was anticipating his next question. He touched her cheek with his fingertips. "Ruth, you've come to mean so much to me. You and Kathryn. I've gone to see the committee. They are in favor of my coming to you. I've got the means to support you and your daughter as well as any children we might have."

Ruth's cheeks paled. She pressed her free hand to her stomach.

"Will you allow me to court you?" Massot took in a breath, waiting for her answer. When he saw tears flood her eyes, his heart sank.

"Oh, Massot. I don't know. I..." she pulled her hand from his and turned away, walking along the edge of the creek. Ruth stared at the water gurgling by.

He followed and stood beside her. "I can support you. I'll take you to the bank and show you my balance.

"I'm not concerned about that. You work hard and always will. It's me. Just me."

Massot waited, allowing her time to think. He prayed that she wouldn't reject him totally. All he wanted was a chance. A chance to court her. To show her what he felt for her. How he would provide for and love both her and Kathryn.

Ruth's gloved hands wiped at her cheeks before she turned to him, twisting her fingers together. "Massot, you are such a wonderful man. You are giving, faithful, wonderful to be around. You've shown me and Kathryn such friendship and caring. I don't want to hurt you in any way. I..." She paused and inhaled, letting the breath out slowly. "You don't know about my background, do you?"

"It doesn't matter, Ruth. Nothing matters but that I care for you. That I'm wanting you for my wife. For Kathryn to be my daughter. I promise I can support you. I've..."

Ruth held up her hand stopping his words. "It's nothing about you. You are wonderful. It's me, what happened to me when I was seventeen." She approached and took his hand. "I don't know if I can be the wife you deserve. A complete wife in every way."

Massot started to speak but she shushed him again.

"When I was young I was very naïve. I didn't pay

attention to anything but what I was interested in. I wandered around my hometown not aware of anyone. A prominent businessman began watching me. He told me so after." Her voice became softer, weaker. "One day, he followed me and was able to grab me from the path and," Ruth swallowed, and cleared her throat. "He... he ... he..."

Massot placed his fingers on her lips. "And you had Kathryn." There was no reason for her to have to say the words. Tears were streaming down her face. Her hand was trembling in his.

"No one believed me. My parents kicked me out. I didn't know what to do. I walked away from my home into the country. I slept in barns as I went. I had no idea where I was going. I bartered for food. I'd clean houses, chicken coops, cattle or horse stalls. Anything so I'd have some food.

"Then Nugget Nate and Penny came along. They took me to Sanctuary Place. I gave birth to Kathryn there. We lived there until we came to Stones Creek. I wasn't sure I should come. I don't know if I can be a wife. It was terrible."

Massot gently, slowly drew her to him and hugged her against his chest. "I'm so sorry you went through that. I suspected something like that happened. It makes no difference to me." He dug in his back pocket and pulled out a handkerchief. He tucked it into her hand.

"Don't you see? If I can't be a wife in all ways, it's not right for me to allow you to court me. Libby or Blanche don't have the same issues that I have."

Massot tipped her chin up. "I don't want Libby or Blanche. I want you. You as my wife. Please let me court you. Let us get to know each other with this intent. If it comes that you can't see me as a husband..." He paused. "Well, I'll respect your wishes. Please, just give me a chance."

Ruth was silent for a long time. She stood trembling in the circle of his arms. They fit together so well. His chin could rest on the top of her head. That she was afraid was evident. Massot wished he could do or say something that would take all the fear and memories away. *Please Lord, help me help Ruth. She's so alone, even with the Ladies and children. I don't think she's ever had anyone to protect her. I understand that what she went through would leave her afraid of men. I want her as my wife. Want to have children with her. Want to raise Kathryn as mine. Please ease her fear. Help me be the one she can be a wife to.*

Ruth tipped her head back and searched his face. "I'll try. If there is any man I trust, it's you. I don't know how long it will take, and I may never feel safe enough, but I'm willing to be courted."

"Thank you. I promise I won't press you. I may ask you occasionally for a decision, but never will I force you in any way." Massot's gaze went back and forth between her eyes. "May I?"

It took a moment for Ruth to understand his question. Red bloomed on her cheeks. Closing her eyes, she nodded.

Softly, gently Massot lowered his lips to hers. He kept the kiss light. He didn't want to do anything that might scare her. That might bring back painful memories. When she relaxed against his chest, the uncertainty eased. The tight band around his heart loosened.

~~~~~

Ruth was distracted the entire time she cleaned Massot's house after he left. The thought of having Massot as a husband was both fascinating and terrifying. He was exactly the type of man she'd want as a spouse; caring, solid, hardworking, dependable. She was attracted to him. Now that he'd made her aware of his intent to court her, unaccustomed desire flared in her middle. Several times she pressed her hands to her belly hoping to still it.

That desire also terrified her. Visions of the man who'd accosted her broke through. The feel of his hands. The pressure of him on top of her. The pain. The laughter as he told of how he'd followed and watched her over the weeks, then walked away, leaving her to pull herself together and go home.

The derision and hateful names her family called her when she told them. The fear that consumed her as she carried a satchel with what they'd allowed her to take when she was forced to leave. Each attacked her mind as she worked. Several times she had to stop cleaning because her hands shook so badly.

Ruth walked slowly back to town, stopping at the edge of the woods. Libby was outside with the twins and Nina. Tadpole sat on the steps, looking bored. The broken arm limited his activities. She was able to keep him at his studies longer.

What was she going to tell the Ladies and children? Especially Kathryn. Her daughter would leap on the idea of her and Massot getting married. Ruth didn't want to tell her, but since Massot would be coming to the House for courting there was no way to keep it from her.

Lunch needed making and Boone and Mae needed

their lessons checked. Ruth couldn't delay any longer. She passed the garden and crossed the street. Nina came running to be picked up and hugged, the twins trailing behind. Tadpole stood up waiting for her. She ruffled his hair.

"I'm bored. I can't do nothin' with his dumb cast." He followed her into the house while Libby herded the twins and Nina.

"Your right arm is perfectly good. We'll do lessons then you can do some weeding this afternoon. Then the others will be home from school by then and you'll have someone to play with. Boone and Mae can weed with you."

"Aww. Weeding's boring too."

"Maybe so, but you want to eat so the garden needs to be weeded. It won't be long before we have radishes and lettuce. Then the peas will be coming on. Brussels sprouts, cabbage, broccoli, they won't be long behind."

"Ain't got a clue what most of them are. Other kids say they ain't worth eatin' anyway." Tadpole shuffled into the wash room to wash before he set the table. He'd found out that having a broken arm didn't exempt him from his normal chores.

Ruth chuckled as he went past her. Soon school would be out for the summer. Several of the boys were around his age and would be available to play with during the day. All the children living in the House who were old enough would be weeding to share the unwelcome chore. Others whose mothers had married would be around also and would help. They wanted to share in the bounty of the House's garden.

Once lunch was over and the little ones put down for naps, Ruth set Tadpole in the room they used as a classroom copying words onto his slate. He was to bring each filled slate for her to check the spelling and penmanship.

Ruth and Libby were in the kitchen when Blanche came in. She sat down at the table and Libby set a cup of coffee in front of her.

"Thank you. My feet hurt. It was a busy day. Almeda's boy, Abe, is sick so she couldn't come to work today. She came in at regular time and did what baking she could, then went home. Thomas stayed with the baby until then. Chloe and I have covered both the bakery and café all morning. Chloe's going to do some of tomorrow's baking this afternoon. That way if the baby is still sick Almeda doesn't have to come in."

Ruth patted Blanche on the shoulder as she moved to another chair with her own coffee cup. Libby finished the supper preparations she was doing, then came and sat with them. Unsure of how to bring up Massot's interest, Ruth listened as her friends chatted.

Laura Duffle came in with a load of laundry. "I decided I wanted to visit with you ladies and iron here instead of in my wash room." Laura was engaged to Hank Johnson the town's barber. She took in laundry as her work. Hank had made one of the back rooms in his shop into a wash room and another for drying. This allowed Laura to do laundry inside when the weather was cold or damp.

"We're glad you did," Blanche said. "Sit and chat and have a cup of coffee before you begin."

Ruth was quiet as the Ladies conversed. It was a while before anyone noticed, but when she didn't laugh at Libby's description of one of Jack's antics they all looked at her.

"What has you so distracted?" Laura asked.

Ruth wrapped her hands around her coffee mug. "Massot asked to court me today."

Each Lady smiled and expressed their delight over the prospect. When they saw her serious expression Blanche placed her hand on Ruth's arm. "He's a good man. What has you so worried?"

Looking at the faces of each of her friends, Ruth took a deep breath. "You all know my past. Since that day I've not wanted to be with a man again. It was awful. Even now, sometimes I wake up at night thinking he's on me. Hurting me."

"Massot would never hurt you," Libby said.

"I know. It's not him. It's me. He's a wonderful man. So caring and giving. He helped Kathryn make my glove box. He is careful never to do anything that would scare me. He's helped in the garden. He helps so many other people in town without asking for anything or mentioning it. Tadpole loves being around him and Massot tolerates him." Ruth smiled and looked down.

"I'm afraid, not of him, but of me. I'm not sure I can be a true wife to him. Afraid every time he touched me I'd think of that man."

"So what are you going to do?" Laura poured more coffee for each of them.

"I told him he could come and court me. He said he'd never press me. He'd let me take as long as I need to decide." She remembered their last moments and could feel her cheeks heat.

"Oh, Ruth. You're blushing." Libby grinned. "What happened to make you blush?"

Ruth pursed her lips and felt herself become even redder. "He hugged me and kissed me when I said he

95

could."

The other ladies were all grinning. "And you liked it?" Laura asked.

Ruth gave a little nod. "It was so gentle. I wasn't at all afraid." She paused. "I liked it."

Smiles stretched the mouths of all three of her friends. She realized they had all been married. Had had loving relationships with their husbands. They knew the joys of the physical side of marriage.

"Am I being foolish to be afraid?"

"It's quite understandable, Ruth," Blanche said. "You went through a terrible experience. One no woman should go through and at such a tender age. You've been protected and out of the sphere of men for years. It's natural for you to be cautious.

"Let Massot court you. Get used to his being with you and touching you, though not too much. I think you'll see your fear fade. Give yourself time and the opportunity to find that you can look forward to being his wife.

"Take all the time you need. If you have questions, ask any of us. If you become uneasy with something, tell Massot. We'll help you understand and I know he'll do whatever he can to ease your fears."

Ruth nodded. It was a good plan. The tightness in her chest released just a little.

"What are you going to tell Kathryn?" Libby asked.

"I'm going to tell her the truth. That Massot asked to court me, that I'm afraid, but I'm going to be courted. My biggest fear in telling her is that she'll latch onto the idea and begin badgering me to decide to marry him. I know she would love to have him as her father. Then if I don't she'll be so disappointed. But I have to tell her. He's going to be coming around and we'll do things together, all three of us."

"There's no hiding being courted around here," Laura said.

"No, there's definitely not. It will be around town too, as soon as the children find out. They blab everything." Everyone laughed at Libby's disgruntled tone. "Then I'll hear about it and be asked about it at the general store. Why not just have it announced at church so most people hear it from Noah. Then they won't have a chance to gossip at me about it."

Ruth grinned and reached across the table. "I'm sorry to be such a terrible problem for you. Shall I ask Ben to raise your wage to cover the distress the biddies of the town cause you?"

More laughter greeted Tadpole as he came into the kitchen with his slate.

"What's so funny?"

"Nothing to concern you," Ruth ruffled his hair.

"Aww, grownups always say that about the good stuff."

~~~~~

Later that evening, Ruth sat behind Kathryn on her bed, brushing her hair. The girl was in her nightgown. They were alone in the room. Mae, who slept in the same room, was in the bathtub.

She'd fallen in a mud puddle after supper, getting not only her clothing dirty but mud had splashed into her face and in her hair. The poor girl, who didn't speak, had cried so hard. Blanche finally understood that Mae was worried about her dress. She was afraid, not only that she would get in trouble for being so dirty but also that the dress wouldn't come clean.

Ozzie Basking, Blanche's thirteen-year-old son, finally convinced her she wasn't in trouble. That these things happened and the Ladies weren't angry; and that if Laura couldn't get the dress clean, someone would make her another one or find one in the trunks where outgrown clothing was stored.

"Kathryn," Ruth began. She was going to explain Massot's intent to court her. She'd been going over how and what to tell her. She didn't want the girl over excited about the prospect of a marriage between them and Massot becoming her father.

Kathryn knew most of the House children were being adopted by the men who married their mothers. Though Kathryn had never seemed to mourn the fact that she never had a father, Ruth suspected she always wanted one. Most of the children from Sanctuary Place didn't have, nor ever had, a father in their past. The few who did rarely spoke of them.

Ruth had told Kathryn about being attacked by a man and that was why she lived at the Place and now the House. Kathryn was born in Sanctuary Place in Dubuque, Iowa. It was the only home she'd known until the move to Stones Creek. She also knew that the Ladies and children had come here to find husbands.

"Massot spoke with me today. He met with the committee and got permission to ask me if he could court me."

Kathryn turned around so swiftly she nearly fell off the bed. "You said yes, didn't you? You're going to get married and Mr. Massot will be my father." She threw her arms around her mother, bouncing with excitement.

"Wait, sweetie, it's not that simple." Ruth hugged

Kathryn to her who pulled back.

"Why not? Mr. Massot's really nice and he likes me. He helped me make the glove box for your birthday." She looked at her mother wide-eyed.

"I've told you about the man who attacked me. Because of that, I'm shy of becoming involved with a man, any man. Massot is very nice. He's kind and good. I like him quite a lot, that's why I'm going to let him court me. I'm hoping to overcome my fears. Hoping that I come to want to be his wife. It may take time."

"How long?"

Ruth smiled and cupped Kathryn's cheek. "I don't know. We will be courting and doing activities together. Some with just him and me, others with all three of us."

Kathryn looked at her mother then placed her hands on her hips. "That will be fun, but just don't take too long to accept him. I want to be able to call him Pa before I'm all grown up."

CHAPTER ELEVEN

"Where's Mae?"

Ruth looked over the dining room. They were getting Sunday dinner on the tables. Everyone had hurried back to the House after church because it was raining. The storm was getting worse by the minute. No one loitered in the church yard.

Blanche looked over the children gathering in the dining room after changing from their good clothes. "I don't see her. Do you suppose she's still upstairs?"

"Ask Kathryn, she's putting rolls in the baskets." Ruth placed platters of ham on the tables. Laura followed with potato casserole.

"I saw her leave the church but haven't seen her since," Laura said.

"Is Mae still upstairs changing?" Blanche asked Kathryn when she brought the baskets from the kitchen.

"Not that I know of. I haven't seen her since church. We sat together, but she hurried out as soon as service was over. I don't think she even waited until Pastor Preston got to the door to greet people."

Blanche wrung her hands together. "Where can she

be?" She hurried out of the room and up the stairs. In a short time she was back again. "I've looked in every room. I don't know where she is. Ozzie, please go and look under the beds and in the closets and don't forget the storerooms. See if Mae is scared of the storm and hiding."

Ozzie, his brother Will, as well as Boone and Tadpole headed up to search. The Ladies kept the other children from following. The younger ones would simply get in the way. The four Ladies stood side by side waiting for them to return, hopefully with Mae.

Ruth pressed her hands to her stomach. Mae was only about ten-years-old. She'd been molested by the men of the King Gang and was still working through her trauma. They didn't know the sound of her voice since she hadn't said a word since she came to live at the House.

Footsteps thundered down the stairs. The boys who'd gone to search for Mae came back without her. Ruth looked at Blanche. She was white as a sheet.

"Where could she be?" Blanche speared Ruth with haunted eyes. "You don't suppose the King Gang came back for her? Stole her right out of the church yard?" She lowered her voice. "Or whoever is watching Kathryn? I don't know what I'd do if something terrible happened to her. She was making such progress becoming more secure here. You don't suppose she ran off, do you?"

Ruth glanced at Laura and gave a small nod toward the children now seated at the tables. Laura nodded back and asked her son Eddie to say grace. Ruth led Blanche into the parlor and closed the doors.

"We don't know what has happened, but we mustn't

scare the other children. I'll go see if I can find her outside and if I can't, I'll go to the jail so a search party can be arranged. You need to stay calm for the others. We don't want them scared and imagining all sorts of awful things."

"You're right. I need to contain my worry so it doesn't spread."

"I'm going to change and get an oilcloth cape. Tell Kathryn I'll be back soon. Tadpole too. He'll ask a million questions. Just say I'm looking for Mae."

She moved to the door but Blanche laid a hand on her arm. "Thank you. She's such a fragile little thing. So much smaller than Kathryn even though they are close in age."

Ruth nodded and went to change.

The rain was coming down harder as she hurried to the church. Maybe Mae had gone back into the building when everyone left so quickly and now was afraid to come home in the storm. Lightning was flashing, followed by deafening thunder.

Pushing the church door open, Ruth went in praying Mae would be on one of the pews or benches. No one was there. She looked under the pews, behind the communion table, the pulpit. The girl wasn't behind the piano either.

Going outside, Ruth got down on her knees to look under the building. Built on foundation blocks, there was room underneath for a man to crawl. Ruth called and looked but Mae wasn't there.

Next she searched more fully around the House. Under the porch, in the alley behind. Even in the wood box. No Mae.

Becoming more worried by the moment, Ruth

decided to report Mae's absence to whoever was working at the jail. They needed more than just Ruth searching for her.

She slogged through the mud, up the street, across, down in front of Doc Eli's clinic, past the blacksmith's, and entered the jail building. Deputy Dak Levine was on duty. He jumped up from his seat behind the desk and came around as Ruth caught her breath.

"What's wrong, Miss Naylor?"

"We can't find Mae. She was with us at church but Kathryn said she ran out just as service ended. We haven't seen her since." Ruth went on telling of the search of the House and her going back to the church. Tears started streaking down Ruth's cheeks. "We're worried the King Gang or someone else may have stolen her."

"Don't go thinking the worst. Are there any children who don't live at the House she might have gone home with?"

"I doubt it. She's not going to school yet. I'm teaching her and the boys. We hope they can get caught up at least partially and can go next fall. She hasn't made friends with the town children yet."

Lightning flashed followed instantly by crashing thunder. Ruth jerked as it startled her. Levine did too.

"You stay here, Miss Naylor. I'll go get the sheriff and see what he wants to do." Deputy Levine pulled on an oilcloth coat and put his Stetson firmly on his head. "Have some coffee to warm yourself. I'll be back shortly." He left just as another bolt of lightning struck.

Ruth ignored his suggestion of coffee and paced the small office. She looked down the hall that was lined with two cells on each side. No one was incarcerated for which she was thankful. Being alone with criminals, even ones locked in jail cells wasn't something she wanted. It reminded her that the King Gang had abandoned the children and were still evading the law.

Though it wasn't long before Sheriff Riverby and Deputy Levine arrived, it felt like an eternity.

"Dak told me that Mae is missing. He explained but I'd like to hear it from you, if you don't mind."

Ruth repeated what she'd told Dak.

Riverby listened carefully, asking her for more details about where she'd searched. "We'll get a search party together now, but we can't go out in this storm. It's too dangerous with all the lightning. Once it breaks we'll begin searching." He pulled out his pocket watch. "It's about one-thirty. It'll take some time to get the word out and get the men back here. Hopefully, the storm will ease up soon. Then we'll head out. How about you head back to the House? I or Deputy Levine will come by and let you know when we start our search."

Ruth wanted to yell that they needed to start the search right now. That Mae had to be terrified even if she hadn't been kidnapped. She held her tongue though. What Sheriff Riverby planned was wise. She didn't want anyone hurt because they were out in the storm.

Instead, Ruth nodded and went back to the House. As she went she prayed for the storm to stop and for Mae to be safe and that Blanche and the rest of the Ladies trusted that God would bring Mae back to them.

~~~~~

The rain didn't seem inclined to let up. Massot sat in his parlor staring out the windows. There weren't any draperies up yet. Ruth never gave him an answer about whether she would make them for him. Maybe she didn't have a sewing machine.

He knew Leah Steele did. She'd brought it to Stones Creek with her when she moved from Kansas, setting up her dress shop. He should probably ask her. He didn't want to burden Ruth if she had to sew them all by hand. His house had many large windows. Massot had hoped to pique Ruth's interest in the house by having her help decorate it. If she accepted his suit, he'd purchase her a sewing machine. And one of those newfangled wringer washing machines that he'd seen in a catalog.

His Bible sat on his lap. He'd been reading. Now he was contemplating what the Word said.

A movement caught his eye. Someone was walking along the creek. What were they doing out in the rain? He realized it wasn't an adult but a child. Massot leaned forward. The child turned, heading to the house. It was Tadpole.

Massot stood and ran down the steps to the first floor and outside, standing under the protection of the second floor. "Tadpole," he hollered. "What are you doing out in the rain like this? Get in here." He waved in a come motion and watched as the boy ran to him.

"Mr. Massot!"

He could hear the desperation in his voice. Tadpole flung himself at Massot who grabbed him up in his arms. "What's wrong?" He carried the boy inside and began stripping the soaking wet clothes from the shivering body. They stuck to his damp cast making them difficult to remove. He needed to get Tadpole warm and dry so he didn't take sick.

"It's Mae. We can't find her. She never came home after church. Stop that." Tadpole began struggling to keep his clothes on. "I gotta go and hunt for Mae. She's my sister, the only family I got."

"You're soaked to the skin. You getting lung fever isn't going to help Mae. Come with me. I'll get some towels and blankets to help you warm up."

Tadpole was shivering so hard he couldn't fight Massot off. Soon he was stripped bare and being wiped dry and wrapped in a quilt. A flour sack towel was folded and tied as a sling for Tadpole's broken arm.

Massot threw more logs into the parlor stove and set Tadpole on the floor near it. "It's hot. Don't touch it." Taking a chair nearby, Massot leaned forward. "Now, tell me what's going on?"

"We all went to church. I saw you there but didn't get any chance to say hi. When we got home we all go up and change out of our Sunday clothes into ones we can get messy in. We was gathering in the dining room for dinner and Mrs. Blanche asked where Mae was. Nobody knew where she was. We were sent upstairs to look for her but nobody found her. Mrs. Blanche was real upset. Miss Ruth went to look for her but didn't find her neither. Then she went to the jail. That's when I went out to look for her. I ain't found her. I gotta go. I gotta hunt for her. What if the gang got her again? They hurt her real bad. That's why she won't talk anymore." He started to unwrap himself from the quilt. "Where's my clothes? I gotta go."

"You stay right there. Answer this for me. Does anyone at the House know you left?"

Tadpole sat and looked at him wide-eyed. "No, I just got my coat and left."

"They're all worried about Mae being missing and you left without saying anything. By now, I'll bet the Ladies and other children are worried about you. You're missing too."

"No, I ain't. I'm right here."

Massot chuckled. "You know where you are, but they don't. Now they have two missing children to worry about."

Tadpole's mouth dropped open. "I never thought of that. I just wanted to find Mae." Tears slid down his face.

"I know, and your intentions were good. Next time be sure to tell someone, an adult, before you head off." Massot stood and ruffled Tadpole's hair. It was damp but not dripping anymore. "I'm going to get one of my shirts and you can wear it back to town. It'll be like a dress but will keep you warm. We'll ride Chester and take your clothes with us. They're too wet for you to wear."

Tadpole struggled to his feet. "You ain't got no clothes my size? At the House we got all sizes from tiny baby clothes clear up to full size. I never seen so many clothes as they've got."

Massot rubbed his fingers across his lips to keep from laughing at Tadpole's statement. The boy had gone from living in an outlaw camp with barely enough to keep warm in to the House that was well supplied with garments for all ages of boys and girls. Most were hand me downs but it still must seem like a treasure trove to him. He might think everyone who lived in town had all those clothes to choose from.

"Nope, I only have clothes my size." Massot went into his bedroom and took a flannel shirt from a drawer. "Like I said. It'll be big, but it'll keep you warm. I've got an extra oilcloth coat I can wrap you in."

It took both of them to get Tadpole into the shirt with all the buttons done right and the sleeves rolled up. Massot got a pair of heavy socks out, put them on his small feet, pulling the cuffs nearly up to Tadpole's knees.

"We're going to ride Chester. That'll get us back to town quicker, you back to the House to let everyone know you are okay and me to the jail to see if a search party is getting together."

They trudged down the stairs. Massot detoured into the kitchen and cut two thick slices of bread, spreading them heavily with creamy butter. He handed one to Tadpole. "Let's eat these before we go. Don't want to head out without putting something in our stomachs."

Tadpole took a big bite. "Nope, that's not a good idea at all," he said with his mouth full.

~~~~~

Ruth hung her oilcloth cape on a hook in the wash room to allow it to drip without trailing it through the House. Blanche came hurrying in.

"Did you find her?"

Ruth wished she could say yes. Blanche was so very worried. It showed in her eyes and the stress lines on her forehead. "No, Blanche, I didn't. Sheriff Riverby is getting a search party together. Once the storm breaks, they'll start searching."

"I'm so scared, Ruth. She was finally not reacting to every little sound. Not hiding behind me when we spoke with people on the street or at church. I was hoping she would begin speaking soon. If she's been taken it will traumatize her all over again." Blanche's hands shook as she pressed them to her mouth to keep from sobbing.

"I understand your fears, but we mustn't let them overtake us. Come, let's have a cup of coffee."

They were silent as they sat at the kitchen table with steaming cups in front of them.

"Mama." Kathryn came into the kitchen. "Have you seen Tadpole? We are starting a game and wondered if he wanted to play."

"Isn't he upstairs with you all?"

"Not that I can find and I looked on both floors."

Ruth and Blanche exchanged glances then stood. They abandoned the coffee and headed to the stairs. Searching each floor and calling his name brought no reply. They asked all the children if they'd seen him leave. No one had.

"He's not in the house. Where is he? Where did he go?" Laura stood with the other Ladies in the hallway on the second floor.

"Maybe he went looking for Mae," Libby said.

Ruth couldn't speak. It seemed her throat was closed by a huge lump. All she could think was that Tadpole and Mae had both been snatched right from under their watchful gazes. Would Kathryn be next? One of the twins? Little Nina?

She looked at Blanche. They hugged each other hoping for comfort.

Someone knocked on the front door. "That must be the sheriff or deputy," Ruth said. "They said someone would come by when they started to search." She hurried down the stairs.

When she pulled open the door, a very wet Massot

carrying an equally wet Tadpole stood there.

"I believe this belongs here." There was a slight lift to one side of Massot's mouth. "I found him wandering in my neck of the woods. Said he was looking for Mae. Has she been found?"

Ruth grabbed Tadpole from his arms and hugged him so tightly he squawked. Ruth pulled back. "I can't believe you left without telling anyone. We were so worried. You knew how worried we are about Mae. Why would you go out in the storm to look for her?"

All the Ladies and children crowded around.

"You went to look for her. I wanted to help. She's all I got as family. She's my sister."

Ruth looked at Massot and set the boy on his feet. "Thank you for bringing him home. No, Mae hasn't been found." She went on to explain about the search party.

"Now that this young'un is home, I'll go join the official search. Try not to worry overmuch, Ladies." His eyes flickered over all those in the foyer then returned to Ruth. "Tadpole's cold and wet." He handed a bundle to her. "These are his wet things. He's got one of my shirts on under the coat and socks. I'll get them another day." Massot knelt down, looking Tadpole in the eye. "You stay here. Don't go looking for Mae on your own. You'll worry the Ladies and other children. Your intentions were good. I know you want to find Mae, but causing more worry isn't the best way to go about it."

Tadpole looked at all the faces around him. They all showed worry. "I'm sorry I worried you all. I just want Mae to be found."

~~~~~

The rain didn't let up. Ruth thought it rained harder, though the lightning and thunder stopped. Deputy Levine came about an hour later saying the men were going to search the town and areas nearby. Stones Creek was rising and would likely escape its banks soon. They wouldn't be able to cross it until it went down.

Blanche told him that when they found Mae or ended the search for the day for the searchers to come for stew and cobbler. Levine tapped the brim of his hat and left.

Myra, Chloe, and Cora came to the House to lend support. Their husbands were searching. Supper came and went. As evening fell the men returned. Without Mae. Ruth and Blanche held each other and cried. Tadpole clung to Ruth. She picked him up letting him cry on her shoulder. All the children were quiet as they prepared for bed. Nina asked to sleep with Kathryn. Soon they were snuggled in bed together.

Ruth stood in the hallway and watched Tadpole toss and turn. Mae was his sister. Ozzie couldn't seem to settle either. Both seemed as worried as the Ladies were for Mae's safety.

The Ladies gathered in the kitchen with cups of tea. None thought they would sleep that night. They sat at the table and prayed that the rain would end, and that Mae was safe and dry and would be returned tomorrow.

~~~~~

Morning was a long time coming. The Ladies had finally gone to bed. Blanche needed to be at the café early. The twins would wake Libby up early. They were too young to understand what was going on. The other children needed to go to school leaving Nina, Tadpole, and Boone waiting in the House. Ruth didn't feel like having lessons and let the children simply do what they wanted for the morning. They sat in the parlor on the settee looking out the window.

Thankfully, the day was sunny and warm. Sheriff Riverby came by saying that the creek was still flooding. It was rushing too fast for anyone to cross. They were going to search further on this side of the creek out from town. Once the water receded they'd cross over and begin searching there.

Laura went to do her laundry across the alley in the back of the barber shop. Libby went to the general store. With Ben participating in the search, it left the entire store in Libby's hands. Ruth kept the twins with her and the others in the parlor. Nina left her vigil and began playing with the twins.

Just as they all sat down to lunch, the back door opened and Blanche ran in carrying Mae. Everyone jumped up, squealing and mobbed them.

"Where?" was all Ruth could ask as Blanche set Mae on her feet.

"She hid in the wagon and went to Hawk's Wing Ranch. They didn't find her until they all got home. By then it was storming too much to bring her home."

The back door opened and Hawk Connor stepped into the wash room. His long black hair hung around his shoulders blanketing his black duster.

"Mr. Connor, please come in. Thank you so much for keeping Mae safe and bringing her back to us." Ruth placed her hand on the man's arm. "Please, join us for lunch. Blanche, can you stay or do you need to go back to the café?"

"I can stay. Chloe and Almeda were going to make me leave anyway. As they said, I've been worthless all morning worrying about this one." Blanche set Mae down, telling her to go wash up. The owner of Hawk's Wing Ranch followed her back to the wash room while the other Ladies set three more places at the tables.

Blanche and Ruth fell into each other's arms, weeping with relief. Mae was home, safe. After lunch they'd send Boone out to let the other Ladies and children know.

CHAPTER TWELVE

The occupants of the House settled back to normal. Mae and Tadpole both had more chores to do than normal. The worry over their actions needed some consequences. Each made sure to let an adult know before going somewhere.

School ended so all the children were home during the day. Often those who had moved out when their mothers married came to play. Ozzie Basking, Blanche's oldest, began working more at the livery stable. It wasn't much work but it brought the boy some money and kept him occupied rather than simply running around town.

Kathryn enjoyed working in the garden and often got up early to weed, hoe, or gather the spring vegetables. Lettuce and radishes graced the tables of the House. Some were sold to the café. There were too many radishes for them to eat.

Ruth sat brushing her hair before she retired when Kathryn came into her room. Climbing up on the bed she studied her mother.

"What, Kathryn?"

"Are you going to marry Mr. Massot?"

Ruth's hand stopped its downward stroke of the brush. "I... I don't know."

"Why not? He wants you to, and I do too."

"It's not that simple. You know why I'm shy around men."

"Mama, that happened a long time ago. Are you going to let it rule your life forever?"

Ruth set the brush down and sat silently looking at the earnest face of her daughter. Hope was written there, as well as disappointment. That tore at Ruth's heart. She didn't want to disappoint her daughter, but her fear was real. The past came back in her dreams even after all those years.

"I found a verse in Philippians." Ruth saw that Kathryn had her Bible in her lap. She opened it and read, "*Brothers, I do not consider myself yet to have taken hold of it. But one thing I do: Forgetting what is behind and pressing toward what is ahead, I press on toward the goal to win the prize for which God has called me heavenward in Christ Jesus.* It says to forget what is in the past and press toward the future. Isn't that right?"

"Yes, Kathryn, it does."

"I know we can't really forget everything. I understand that. But should it keep us from winning the prize God has for us? Mama, what if that prize is Mr. Massot?"

Ruth let her daughter's words of faith wash over her. Was she holding on to the past and keeping herself from blessings God had waiting for her? She didn't know, but she knew what she did have to do. She needed to turn her fears over to God for fear was not of Him.

Stroking Kathryn's hair, Ruth gave a small smile.

"You've given me a lot to think about. Also a lot to pray about." She leaned forward and kissed her daughter's cheek. "Thank you."

Kathryn went to the room she shared with Mae and Ruth took her Bible, opening it to the place the ribbon bookmarked. As she read Psalm 91 two verses spoke to her heart. *He who dwells in the secret place of the Most High will rest in the shadow of the Almighty. He will cover you with his feathers. Under his wings you will take refuge. His faithfulness is your shield and rampart.*

Had she been dwelling in the Lord's secret place, resting in His shadow? Was she allowing Him to cover her with His wings? Was she taking refuge in Him? Or was she allowing fear from her past to keep her from His protectiveness? From the blessing of a man who wanted to shelter and protect her. From someone who might grow to love her and her daughter. From her being a blessing to his life.

Turning down the lantern, Ruth lay in the dark releasing her fears and memories to the One who could give her refuge from them.

~~~~~

Massot dumped the bucket of manure he'd shoveled from Chester's stall on the pile he was making away from the house. Most of the time it was downwind. Once it went through the winter he'd turn it into the soil he planned to use for his garden. He hoped by next spring Ruth and Kathryn would help put the garden in. As he'd promised, Massot hadn't pressured her.

They were courting but it seemed extremely slow to him. He'd stop by most days after he finished work. They might only chat for a few minutes since she often was busy with getting supper. He hadn't figured out the schedule of which days she didn't have supper duties.

Kathryn was always happy to see him, as was Tadpole, though he'd been a little shy since he'd gone searching for Mae without letting anyone know. Massot was trying to get the boy at ease with him again. He liked Tadpole. The boy was certainly precocious.

Massot returned the bucket to the hook on the wall of the small horse shed, and patted Chester on the nose when he came over to the fence of the small corral attached to the shed. Maybe he'd come home early and take the horse for a ride. With the good weather, Massot was working long hours and didn't take time to exercise the horse very much. Rising with the sun, he took full advantage of the longer days.

He was nearly ready to head to town. There were just the finishing touches to put on the Steele house. The family should be able to move in by the following week. Four would move into the apartment above the dress shop. Then he'd begin McIlroy's house.

As he walked across to the house, Massot heard scuffling, then a scream. It was either a woman or child's voice. Lifting his head, he scanned the woods trying to locate the direction the sounds were coming from.

More scuffling, a male grunt, then the sound of a slap. Now able to identify where the noises were originating, Massot ran in that direction. Not knowing what or who he'd find, he slipped the trigger thong off his gun.

Running up a rise that dropped off on the other side, Massot growled when he saw who was in the hollow.

Ira Bragg had a hold of Kathryn who was kicking and swinging with her free arm. The bodice of her dress was torn, making Massot even angrier. That Ira had a bloody nose pleased him, but not enough to restrict his leap from the top of the rise onto the man, knocking him from Kathryn. The men landed sprawled in the debris on the forest floor.

Massot jumped up and grabbed Ira by the shirt front. Hauling him up, Massot swung his fist into Ira's jaw sending him flying back. The man hit the trunk of a tree and sank in a heap.

Kathryn was crying but grabbed onto Massot when he reached for her.

"Are you all right, sweetheart?" Massot brushed leaves and twigs from her dress as she cried against his chest. He waited until her sobs subsided then pulled back so he could look at her.

"He... he... I... wa... was weeding the garden, and then he grabbed me, running into the woods. I tried to get away but he was too strong. He said he was going to..." She broke into sobs again.

Massot wrapped his arms around her. "It's okay. I'm here. You're safe. I won't let anything happen to you. I'll take you home."

The sound of Ira getting up made Massot turn. He started to go after the fleeing man but Kathryn held onto him.

"Don't leave me."

Massot watched as Ira ran through the woods disappearing in the trees. He didn't like letting him get away, but Kathryn's needs came first. Her breaths were coming in shallow hiccups.

"Come on, honey. Let's get you home. Do you want

to walk or ride with me on Chester?" He wrapped an arm around her shoulders and began guiding her up the rise.

"W...walk. I need to catch my breath before I see Mama. This will scare her so badly."

"It will, but I got to you in time. He wasn't able to do more than tear your dress, was he?" If she'd suffered more than that, he'd be on Chester so fast, combing the hills until he found the little... Massot bit off the word. He knew if he found him no one else ever would.

They walked slowly back to town. He stopped her just before they could be seen from the House. He'd given her his handkerchief earlier. Now, he inspected her face. It was obvious she'd been crying and there was a haunted look in her eyes.

Massot wrapped his arms around her again, pressing her head against his chest. "I'm proud of you. You fought him as well as you could. He was bleeding when I got there."

Kathryn gave a little grin. "I smashed his nose with my fist. Twice. I wasn't going to let him do anything to me without fighting back. I've lived with all those boys my whole life. I know a thing or two about fighting."

Massot held the chuckle in. "You ready to see your mother? She's going to be upset that this happened to you."

"I know. I'm ready. I need to see her." Tears filled Kathryn's eyes again and Massot knew she'd break down as soon as she saw Ruth.

~~~~~

"You head on up to the school room, Tadpole. I want to see you copy those pages again." Ruth shooed the boy up the stairs, his slate rubbing against his trousers transferring the chalk onto them. She ignored his grumbling. Seems he thought that what he'd done the day before was good enough. Ruth disagreed.

A knock sounded and she turned to answer the door. Massot stood there with Kathryn who burst into tears and grabbed her around the waist, holding on for dear life.

"What?" Ruth looked from her daughter to Massot.

"Let's go into the parlor. Kathryn's had a fright." Massot's gravelly voice was more pronounced than usual. He closed the door when they went in. Ruth and Kathryn sat on the settee. Massot stood.

"I was outside my house and heard a scream. I followed it and found Ira Bragg dragging Kathryn. She was fighting for all she was worth. He was bleeding. I got him away from her. Once we calmed down, we walked to town. She's..."

Ruth didn't let him finish. "Oh Lord, no, Kathryn, are you all right?" She'd cupped Kathryn's cheeks in her hands. There were small scrapes on her face. When Kathryn wiped her tears she saw more on her hands. There was blood on the cuff of her sleeve.

"He tried, but he didn't hurt me. He's the one who's been watching me. He said so. I kicked and smashed him in the face." She stopped. "I was scared."

Ruth hugged her again. "I'm sure you were." Kathryn snuggled into her arms. She looked at Massot.

"Ruth, he got away. I knocked him down and I thought he was out. I was comforting Kathryn and he got up and ran away. I'm sorry."

"Oh, Massot. Don't be. You saved her. He'll be found. We'll get the sheriff to get a posse together. He

121

shouldn't be that hard to find."

A knock on the door was followed by Tadpole sticking his head in the room. "I got the sentences." He stopped when he saw Kathryn. "What happened?" He pushed the door open and came in.

Ruth glanced at Massot who merely twitched a smile.

"Kathryn had a scare. Set your slate down. I'll look at it in a little while. Would you do a favor for me? Please go find the sheriff and ask him to come here."

Tadpole's eyes got rounder. "Gotta be serious if you want the sheriff." He looked from Kathryn to Ruth then Massot. He ran out of the room. The front door slammed and he was running across the yard to the street.

"Do I have to talk to the sheriff?" Kathryn lifted her head. Her eyes were red and puffy. There were dark smudges under them.

Ruth looked at Massot. He gave a small shake of his head. "No, honey. At least not today. He may want to ask you some questions but not today. I'll take you upstairs and help you change out of this." They stood and Ruth nodded her head at Massot then at the settee, indicating that he should stay. He nodded. She could feel his eyes on her back as she and Kathryn left the parlor.

~~~~~

Ruth's hands were shaking as she helped Kathryn into her nightgown and tucked her into bed. Libby wasn't working at the store today and what had happened shocked her when Ruth explained.

Mae came in and sat on the bed, patting her friend on the back. Mae knew all too well what could have happened to Kathryn if Massot hadn't found her.

"Will you stay with her, Mae? I need to go downstairs and meet with Sheriff Riverby."

Mae nodded, bent over and took off her shoes. Then she crawled under the blankets. Kathryn snuggled against Mae, who smiled up at Ruth. She was so pleased to be able to help.

Ruth closed the door as she left, giving both girls kisses. Libby met her in the hall and descended the stairs with her.

"Is she all right? She was so white."

"I hope so. I hope they can catch that..." Ruth bit her lip. Calling the man a bad name wouldn't help.

"Me too. I don't think any of us will feel at ease until he is." Libby put a hand on Ruth's arm as they reached the first floor. "Most of the boys are out playing. They were going to the school yard to play some ball. I'll keep the twins and Nina out of the parlor. I'll fix lunch also. Don't worry about it."

"Thank you. We'll need to tell all the children but not until I speak with the sheriff."

Libby hugged Ruth. "I wish this hadn't happened. I know she wasn't hurt physically but emotionally it had to be terrible."

"She was glad she was able to bloody his nose. That she could will hopefully give her some satisfaction."

The front door flew open, nearly hitting the Ladies. Tadpole ran in, stopping suddenly when he noticed them.

"I brung Sheriff Riverby. He's hopping mad. Said some bad words. I told him he'll get in trouble if he uses them. Can I go tell the others what happened?"

"No," both Ruth and Libby said at the same time.

"I need you to help with the little ones. We'll tell

them later. No sense ruining their morning." Libby placed a hand on his shoulder and guided Tadpole into the dining room.

Sheriff Riverby stood just inside the door, his hat in his hands. "I'm real sorry this happened to your daughter, Miss Naylor. Is she all right?"

"Thank you. I hope so. She's resting. Mae is with her. Come, Massot is in the parlor. We'll talk there."

It didn't take long for Massot to relate what happened. The grim faces of the men showed Ruth how seriously they took the incident.

"I'm going to put a posse together and search. I'm not real confident we'll find him. We've not been able to locate the King Gang. Ira knows the area too. Knows places to hide. I'll search his room at the rail station too. He lives there so he can get telegrams in the night. Looks like we'll be needing a new station master and telegraph operator."

"I'll be on that posse, Sheriff." Massot stood and turned to Ruth who was sitting on the settee next to him. "I'll come around later and let you know what's happening. I want to see Kathryn too. Let her know she's safe."

Ruth nodded. She was exhausted from her emotions. Worry about the safety of Kathryn, Mae, as well as the other children and Ladies weighed heavily on her.

"I'm going to suggest that none of the children go out alone. Especially Kathryn and Mae. We don't want a repeat of this morning," Sheriff Riverby said. "It might be best if Boone, Ozzie or one of the other boys is with the girls until we catch Ira. Just to be on the safe side."

Massot nodded, spearing Ruth with a somber look. Again, all Ruth could do was nod.

~~~~~

Mae came downstairs a couple of hours after Massot and Sheriff Riverby left. She pulled on Ruth's arm indicating that Kathryn was awake and wanting to see her.

Climbing the stairs slowly, Ruth prayed her daughter wouldn't be too traumatized by Ira's attempted kidnapping. She sent up prayers of thanks that Massot was near enough to hear the struggle and come to the rescue. There was no doubt he cared deeply for Kathryn as she did for him. He'd make a good father.

Was that enough for Ruth to set aside her misgivings and marry him? There was a conflict within her. One moment she was positive she should accept Massot's suit. The next, anxiety would flood through, tearing the concept apart. She set the matter aside as she entered Kathryn's bedroom.

Kathryn was dressing, which surprised Ruth. She thought the girl would stay in bed the rest of the day.

"How are you, honey?" Ruth searched her daughter's face.

"I'm good. The nap helped. Having Mae here did too. I knew you had to talk with the sheriff and I wasn't alone."

"Do you want to tell me about it?"

Kathryn gave a wan smile. "I was scared, but I fought really hard. I was so glad when Massot knocked him away from me. He wanted to chase after Mr. Bragg but I didn't want him to leave me." Kathryn finished buttoning her bodice and looked at Ruth. "Have they found him?"

Ruth left out a soft breath. "No, honey, they haven't. At least not yet." She went on to explain the posse and the suggestions Sheriff Riverby had made about the children staying together and watching out for the girls.

Kathryn nodded, then grinned. "I bet the boys hate that."

Ruth chuckled. "They did complain some, but once they understood what happened and how scared you were they decided they could do that."

"I'm hungry. I missed lunch, didn't I? Mae too."

"Libby is getting you both some food. Let's go down and get you fed." As Kathryn stepped into the hall, Ruth said, "Are you still scared?"

"No, Mama, fear is not of God. I'm not going to let being afraid keep me from having fun and doing what I want. I trust that God will protect me. It's in Psalm 91:4. Pastor preached on it a few weeks ago. I memorized it. *He will cover you with His feathers; you will take refuge under His wings. His faithfulness will be a protective shield.* I know He'll protect me.

"Mr. Bragg will be found sometime soon. I'm not going to let him take the joy from my life."

Kathryn ran to the stairs and clumped down as fast as she could. Ruth followed more slowly.

CHAPTER THIRTEEN

A few days later, Ruth was mending in the dining room. Libby was sewing something for the twins and Blanche was drinking a cup of tea. She'd just returned from working in the café. A knock sounded on the front door. Blanche got up to answer it.

Ruth could see it was Sheriff Riverby and set her mending aside and rose. Maybe he had news of Ira Bragg who hadn't been found. His room at the station had been empty when they searched it. Seems he wasn't planning on returning to Stones Creek when he kidnapped Kathryn.

"Afternoon, Sheriff. What can I do for you?" Blanche held the door open so he could enter.

Newt tipped his hat. "Ma'am. I've got three women here who're needing what this house gives — sanctuary. They escaped the King Gang yesterday and walked to town. Not sure how far it was, but I'm sure they need food and shelter. Will…"

Blanche cut him off. "Of course, come in." She brushed Newt aside and gently pulled the women into the house. "Come to the kitchen. We'll…"

Tadpole, Mae, and Boone pushed past Ruth in their

127

hurry to get to the women, hugging them with all their might.

The back door slammed, and Chloe ran into the room. "Flora. Sally. Oh my word, Ada. Praise the Lord." She hugged one, then another, then the last, repeating the hugs several times.

Soon they were sitting at the table, bowls of rich stew in front of the newcomers. Sally Rife, a short woman with hair that might be blonde once it was washed had asked about her daughter Nina. Libby had taken her upstairs to see the child as she napped. Sally was eager to see her but didn't want to wake her up.

Flora Potter was tall and big boned. Both of her children had died in the measles epidemic. There was a sadness in her eyes that Ruth longed to ease.

Ada was Boone's older sister. Rather than leave her with the other children, the men decided she was old enough to use and abuse as they did all the women. She was fourteen. Ruth wanted to wrap the girl in her arms and help take away all the pain. She looked at the women and knew they'd all suffered the same. Ruth understood a little, but Chloe McIlroy understood so much more. She'd been kidnapped at age ten and lived with the gang until they abandoned her and her son Duncan when she was about to give birth to Lil Pen.

Nina was overjoyed to see her mother again, when she woke up from her nap. She expressed the feelings of the children and the women when she said, "I no want to go back, Mama. Want to stay here. I gots a bed and lots to eat. Pretty dress."

Sally kissed Nina. "I don't want to go back either. I want to stay here, too."

~~~~~

Massot stood holding Chester's reins as Sheriff Riverby and Nugget Nate Ryder argued. Nate and his wife Penny had arrived a couple of days earlier.

They were Ben Cutler's uncle and aunt. Nugget Nate was a crusty man from the mountains of Kentucky. He'd made a fortune when he found a gold mine in New Mexico years before. He was the man who sponsored Sanctuary Place and Sanctuary House, though those who knew them well knew Penny was truly in charge of their marriage and many of the philanthropic endeavors the couple were involved in.

Nate and Riverby had spent the last couple of days arguing on how the search for the King Gang was going to be carried out. Finally, Riverby allowed Nate to scout for the outlaw camp. Now, Riverby was explaining who would stay in town and where they would be guarding and who was going with the posse.

"You's about done jawin', Sheriff? I'm a thinkin' we's a needin' ta be headin' out. We's burnin' daylight." Nugget Nate straightened from leaning against the jail wall.

"Yeah, Nate. I think we've covered everything."

Massot mounted. He'd stopped by the House to speak with Ruth and Kathryn. All the Ladies were scared. Four and Hank Johnson were guarding the House. Several other men were stationed around town in case the outlaws came while the posse was out.

"You be careful, Massot." Ruth had looked up at him with such worry in her eyes he'd had difficulty not wrapping his arms around her and not letting go. Kathryn had clung to him as he said good-bye as well.

"Let's ride," Riverby hollered. The men of the posse set their horses to a gallop, Nugget Nate in the lead as he'd found the camp of the King Gang earlier in the morning.

~~~~~

Ruth sat on a bed in the room several boys slept in on the third floor. It was to the back of the House. Hank Johnson and the lawyer called Four had instructed everyone to stay there. Kathryn sat on one side of her, Tadpole on the other.

The waiting was horrible. The gang must know that the women who'd escaped and the children they'd abandoned were living there. The House would be a target. The older children understood what was going on and what could happen. The littler ones couldn't and weren't happy to have to stay in the stuffy room with the doors and windows closed. The room was large but with so many people it was hot. No one had thought to bring water or snacks upstairs.

The Ladies spent time praying and then explaining to the three women about God. None knew much and what they did know was a jumbled mess of ideas.

The twins and Nina had fallen asleep as it was their normal nap time.

"I need to use the necessary," Tadpole complained. "I can't hold it no more."

Ruth pointed to the chamber pot in the corner.

Tadpole stood with his hands on his hips. "I ain't gonna go in there with all these girls in here."

"Then I guess you're going to hold it since you aren't leaving the room." Ruth wasn't going to risk him wandering off to find Hank or Four who were watching from the front windows.

Tadpole twisted his mouth in irritation which changed to jaw dropping shock when gunshots began firing both in front of the House and in the Main Street. He dove into Ruth's lap.

Everyone dropped to the floor and slid under the beds. Hank had instructed that it would be safest for them there. The twins and Nina started crying, startled from their naps at the loud sounds. Libby held one of her toddlers, Flora wiggled under the bed with her and the other one.

The shooting went on and on. Kathryn, pressed against Ruth, holding her tight around her waist. Tadpole did the same on the other side.

All Ruth could think about was Massot. She knew he'd be in the thick of the fighting. He was just that dedicated a man to want to make sure the outlaws were stopped. He'd do whatever was necessary, even give his own life if it came to that.

He might die. Killed by a bullet fired by a criminal who cared nothing about anyone. Ruth's heart squeezed so tightly in her chest she nearly couldn't breathe. She might lose him. Never see his lopsided grin. Never hear the gravelly voice again. Never have a chance to tell him she loved him.

The realization that she loved Massot came hard in the tight, dusty space under the bed. Tears gathered. As she lay there with her arms around Kathryn and Tadpole, Ruth knew her fear of a man was nothing compared to the fear of losing the man she loved.

~~~~~

Massot helped gather up the bodies and wounded outlaws. God had been gracious and none of the posse or townsfolk were killed or severely injured. Doc Eli was tending to them. The injured of the King Gang would be treated once everyone else was.

The Ladies of Sanctuary House had instructed the posse to come and get a meal they had prepared once everything was settled. Massot was hungry, but that wasn't why he wanted to go to the House.

No word of injuries to townsfolk was brought by Four or Hank which relieved his worry for the women and children. Massot and Red Dickerson, foreman at Hawk's Wing Ranch had fought in the street in front of and the alley behind the House.

At Sheriff Riverby's call releasing the posse, Massot hurried down the street between the House and dress shop. As he rounded the corner, the door opened and Ruth ran out and down the porch steps. She crossed the yard, coming straight toward him. Her arms were outstretched and she grabbed him in a big hug.

"Oh, Massot. You're all right. I was so scared. More scared than I've ever been in my life. I was so afraid you would be killed." She began covering his face with kisses. "I couldn't stand it if you had been shot." She kissed him again. "I'm so thankful you're okay. You are okay, aren't you? I don't see any blood or bandages. Red was injured and Gema ran to Doc's office. Is he okay? I'm so glad you all won. I was so very scared I'd never get the chance to tell you I love you. Will you marry me? Please say yes." She sprinkled more kisses on his face, then opened her mouth to begin talking again. Massot took the opportunity to keep her quiet by cradling her face in his hands and pressing his lips to hers and not letting go.

Against her lips, he said, "Yes."

When he released her and gazed into her eyes, Ruth asked, "Yes, what?"

"Yes, I'll marry you. Yes, I love you. Yes, I'm fine."

His Protective Wings

CHAPTER FOURTEEN

Kathryn was ecstatic. She jumped and threw her arms around Massot asking if she could call him Papa. As she chattered excitedly, he decided she got her babbling ability from her mother.

He and Ruth had taken Kathryn across to his building and up to the apartment. They didn't want to discuss their upcoming nuptials at the House where they might become the center of attention and not be able to celebrate as the new family they were becoming.

They decided to make the announcement the following day. Today had been both upsetting and exciting. Though their news was good, they didn't want it to be overshadowed by the killing and injuries.

They were still in the apartment. Massot took Kathryn's hands. "I have some more news for you. Ira Bragg had joined up with the King Gang. He was killed in the shootout. You don't have to worry about him coming for you anymore."

First delight, then sadness flitted across her features. "I'm glad that he can't get me, but I'm sorry he got killed. Now he can't be forgiven by accepting Jesus."

135

Massot drew her against him. "That's very forgiving of you. Many people wouldn't think that way."

"Maybe not, but I want to be forgiven so I have to forgive. The Bible and Pastor Noah say that."

"Yes, they do." He hugged her then let her go. "How about we go get some of that food you Ladies promised the posse?"

Kathryn bounced as Ruth and Massot looked on. "I'm not sure I can keep this a secret. I'm so happy."

"How about pretending it's a Christmas present? And it's only until tomorrow," Ruth smiled and laid a gentle hand on Kathryn's shoulder.

"Oh, all right. If I must, but only until tomorrow. I just know I'll bust if I have to keep it in any longer."

Kathryn ran down the stairs. Massot took the opportunity to kiss Ruth again.

~~~~~

Kathryn was still bouncy the next day and Ruth had to remind her not to give away their secret. She'd told Libby, Laura, and Blanche that Massot was coming to supper that evening. The ladies had smiled at her as if they suspected something but didn't say anything. Hank Johnson would be there too. Since he and Laura had become engaged back in March, Hank was a regular at supper.

Tadpole was excited about Massot coming too. He idolized the man and was over at the shop whenever he knew Massot was there.

Ruth watched him trying to play catch with one hand. His summer was going to be limited with his cast on. There would be no swimming, playing ball wasn't looking too promising either since he dropped the ball more than he caught it.

Massot appeared, carrying tools as he headed to his shop. Tadpole abandoned the game, running to greet him. Ruth watched the interplay between the two. Massot gave one of his rare broad smiles and ruffled Tadpole's hair. The boy now carried a hammer, though he'd acted like he wanted to carry the saw.

Ruth smiled and went into the House to continue supper preparations. Sally was watching the twins and Nina play on the porch while Libby worked at the general store. Blanche was in the kitchen.

"I see you made a cake today, Ruth," Blanche said. "Any special reason?"

Ruth knew Blanche was hinting at something and suspected Kathryn may not have been able to keep the secret.

"Celebrating the end of the King Gang, Blanche. We don't have to worry about them or Ira Bragg anymore. I hate the deaths but am glad their reign of terror is ended."

"I agree." When Blanche winked, Ruth was sure the beans had been spilled.

They worked on supper and when the front screen door began slamming shut over and over she knew the children were traipsing in. Ruth and Blanche looked at each other and shook their heads, smiling.

Tadpole came running into the kitchen, his cast banging on the doorframe. "Mr. Massot is here. I helped him put his tools away. He's been working on Doc Steele's house. It's just about done. He says they can move in next week. Then that lawyer is moving into their apartment. Can I help with all the moving?"

"I don't know, Tadpole. You'll have to ask Doc or Mr. Farnsworth."

"That ain't his name. It's Mr. Four." Tadpole ran into the wash room. He had supper duties that night.

Ruth decided not to correct him. He'd never remember anyway. Everyone was calling the lawyer Four, so Mr. Four worked well. It had taken long enough to get Tadpole to remember the title when speaking to grownups, at least now he was using them.

Massot stuck his head in the kitchen. "Anything I can help with?" His gravelly voice sent shivers up Ruth's spine. Rather than fear, they brought on unfamiliar yearnings. She looked at Blanche who grinned.

Ruth was saved from replying by Hank and Laura coming in through the back door. It was time to start taking food into the dining room. She handed a large bowl filled with green beans to Massot, feeling herself blush.

It wasn't long before everyone was eating and sharing their activities of the day.

When dessert was served, Massot stood up. "I've got an announcement."

Blanche grinned, looking straight at Ruth.

"Nugget Nate came by today. He's having a party Saturday evening at the warehouse. It's going to be what he calls a hoedown. There'll be food, which everyone can contribute to, and music and dancing. It's for everyone, both young and adult."

The children all cheered.

"Another thing. Ruth has agreed to marry me. We haven't set a date but," he looked straight at her as he took her hand, drawing her to her feet. "It's not going to be long."

All the Ladies jumped up and surrounded Ruth,

hugging and congratulating her. Massot stayed close to her, though Kathryn wormed her way into his embrace, smiling up at him.

~~~~~

Once the excitement of the announcement of their engagement was over, things settled down to a normal routine. The new ladies from the King Gang were responsible for the dishes with the children's help.

Laura and Hank came to Ruth and Massot asking them to come talk out on the porch. The early June evening was warm and long. Most of the children were in the yard playing. Hank and Laura sat on the porch swing while Ruth and Massot sat in wicker chairs. Massot had placed his close to hers and held her hand. Hank had his arm stretched behind Laura's back.

"Massot, Ruth," Hank began. "Congratulations. I'd recommend a short time before your wedding too. We've waited since March and, in my opinion, it's been too long."

Laura swatted him softly on the arm. "Stop that. What we were wondering is whether you two would like to have a double wedding with us? You know it's on the twenty-sixth."

Massot's smile stretched across his face. Ruth was a little shocked, but when she looked at him and saw how the idea pleased him, she grinned and nodded.

CHAPTER FIFTEEN

The warehouse next to the railroad tracks had been cleaned and a large space had been created by moving everything to the sides. A platform was along the back wall and a number of Stones Creek residents played instruments so others could dance.

Nugget Nate had purchased food from the hotel and café and the women had all contributed. There were two tables of drinks. One was available to all. The other restricted to adults. Several of the youth had tried to sneak sips but Mrs. Fugard kept an eye on that table.

Massot was standing alongside of the dancing, watching Ruth dance with Tadpole. The boy had been sullen the last couple of days and she was trying to cheer him up.

"Massot," Nugget Nate said as he stepped up beside him. "How's ya doin'?"

"Doing well, Nate. Your Penny and Gema Dickerson sounded real good on those fiddles," Massot replied.

"Don't go callin' it a fiddle. Penny gets mighty riled up iffen I do. It be a violin." The way he said the word in an attempted sophisticated manner made Massot chuckle.

Nate looked at him squinting one eye. "Ya ain't as growly as I remember ya ta be. What's caused that?"

Massot nodded toward Ruth. "Miss Naylor and I are getting married in a couple of weeks. Double wedding with Hank Johnson and Mrs. Duffle."

Nate smacked Massot on the back. "Congratulations. I knowed about Hank and Laura. Ain't heard a nothin' 'bout you an' Ruth."

"Just decided. Hank suggested we get married at the same time. We thought it would be a fine time to tie the knot."

"Ya gonna live above your shop?"

"No, I have a house about fifteen minutes' walk." Massot pointed in the direction. "Built it over a couple of seasons. Moved in a while back. Has space for Kathryn and any other children we may have."

Nate was silent for a moment. "Ya built most of the buildings here in town, ain't ya? That be what I'm wanting' ta jaw with ya about."

Massot lifted his eyebrows and studied Nate. "Oh?"

"Yep, I'm wonderin' iffen ya'd be interested in helpin' me with a project."

"I'm pretty booked up. I have several houses lined up to build."

"That's what I be talkin' 'bout. I'm aimin' ta hire up some men ta come ta town an' get them houses built faster. Town's growin', an' not just with the House Ladies. There be a need for more houses than what ya can do on yer own.

"I got some young men who need a place ta get some experience. They come from trouble, but want ta work honest. All be God fearin' an' know how ta work.

142

Thought ya'd make a good foreman for the crew. Ya'd do the managin' an' ramrodin'. Houses would get built quicker and that'll attract more businesses ta town.

"I'd be payin' ya good, iffen yer interested?"

"Haven't ever thought of something like that. Always just hired day labor when I need help."

"Well, ya think on it an' let me know. I'm a plannin' on stayin' in Stones Creek fer a while. God ain't done with me here, yet."

"I'll do that. Need to discuss it with Ruth."

Nate slapped Massot on the back. "I done knowed ya was a smart man. Cornsultin' yer woman afore ya make a decision. Some men never learn that, an' here ya are doin' it an' ya ain't even married yet.

"Come on. Let's celebrate yer upcomin' nuptials with some of my squeezin's."

Massot took a last look at Ruth, then followed Nate to the adult libation table.

~~~~~

Ruth was worried about Tadpole. He'd been despondent since the shootout. Or rather after she and Massot had announced their coming marriage. He wasn't the happy child he'd become since arriving at Sanctuary House. He'd stopped talking about choosing a birthday.

She'd tried to cheer him up by paying special attention to him. They'd danced at the party, but now he was sitting along the wall with his knees up, the cast across them with his chin resting on it.

Evening was progressing as Massot came bringing a glass of punch. "Here, it's from the non-spiked table."

"Thank you."

Massot told her of the offer Nate had made, saying

he was only mentioning it now. They could discuss it later. "You don't look like you are having a good time. I'm not a good dancer, but if you want, I'll take a turn around the room with you." He leaned down and whispered, "It's the only way I can hold you without raising eyebrows."

Ruth looked up at his face. No fear flooded her. Not even a speck. She felt totally safe with him. She felt other sensations too, but those couldn't be explored until after the wedding.

"We don't have to. I'm having a good time, it's just... I'm worried about Tadpole. He seems so sad. He's not participating much. Not at home or here at the party. See, the other children are all running around, playing, and dancing. He's just sitting there."

"Do you think it's because of his arm?" Massot asked.

"I know what it is." Kathryn wrapped her arm around Massot's waist. She was so looking forward to having him as a father. "He's upset because Mama and I will be leaving the House when you get married. He doesn't think we'll even remember him or want to visit."

Ruth and Massot looked at each other. It had never occurred to them that Tadpole was that attached.

Libby came up holding onto the hands of the twins. "It's getting late. I'm taking these two back to the House and putting them to bed. It will be hard enough getting them up for church tomorrow."

"I'll take one," Kathryn said. "I'm ready to go too. I'll see if Tadpole wants to go. He doesn't look like he cares to stay." She picked up Jack and went to speak with Tadpole. Ruth and Massot watched the group leave. Other families were gathering their children to head home too.

"Let's take a walk, Ruth. We can take the long way back to the House."

Ruth nodded and they set their glasses on the table and slipped out a side door. Massot placed her hand on his elbow and kept his other hand on hers. They walked in silence along the railroad tracks.

"Massot, what are we going to do about Tadpole? I hate that he's so upset over our marriage."

When his silence stretched long, Ruth worried that he would say it wasn't any of their concern.

Massot stopped and turned to face her. "I have a suggestion, but I don't know if you will want it."

"What?" Ruth knew what she wanted to do.

"Tadpole is a smart, fun little boy. He has some rough edges, which are understandable. What he needs to help polish those is a loving family.

"I'm fond of the boy. I know you care more than a little for him. Kathryn too. I think he feels the same towards you. He seems to like and listen to me.

"How about we see if he'd like for us to adopt him? Mae too, if she wants."

Ruth flung herself into his arms and kissed him. "That's what I was hoping you'd say. I love that little guy like he was my own. That was the one thing I wasn't looking forward to about our marriage, leaving him behind."

"Why didn't you say anything?" Massot asked.

"Everything's happened so quickly, there hasn't been time. I was planning to."

Massot held her close against his chest. "My life is certainly changing fast. Getting married, suddenly having children. Possibly a job supervising construction of several homes at the same time." He tipped her chin up and looked into her eyes. "I never dreamed I'd be someone a woman would want to marry. Now I have you. You're the one who will make it possible for all those things to happen. I love you."

Ruth grinned. "I love you too. You can do it all. I know you can."

~~~~~

They had discussed the children and Nate's offer late into the night, sitting on the porch swing of the House. Massot was planning to accept the job once all the details were worked out.

Tadpole, they thought, would jump at the chance to be adopted. As they thought about the weeks he'd been at the House, it became clear he looked to Ruth as a mother and was starting to place Massot in the role of a father.

Mae, on the other hand, was a question. It was obvious she loved her brother. The ties she was developing went more toward Blanche and her children. Blanche was who she turned to when there were problems or when she was afraid. She liked playing with Nancy who was younger than Mae. Nancy was still interested in dolls which Mae had never had.

The girl still didn't speak and no one was pushing her. Mae had been through such abuse, no one wanted to force her and place more of a burden on her than necessary.

She was also drawn to Hawk Connor, as her hiding in their wagon and going to the ranch showed.

Ruth and Massot would offer to adopt Mae to keep

her with Tadpole, but would let her make her own decision. The children would be near each other even if Mae didn't want to be adopted. They would make sure she knew she was welcome. Also, if Mae chose to stay at the House, no one would be upset.

Church service was over and they were all walking home. Tadpole lagged behind, kicking at the dusty street as he went. Ruth was eager to talk with him, but they were going to wait until after the noon meal.

As soon as all the dishes were washed and those children who had meal chores dismissed, Massot asked Tadpole and Mae to join he and Ruth in the parlor. Kathryn was there also, though she hadn't been told what was going to happen.

"You know that Ruth and I are getting married at the same time Hank and Laura are. Ruth and Kathryn will be moving in with me at my house in the woods.

"Ruth and I care for you deeply and are willing to adopt you if you'd like that. We'd be your parents, legally, and no one could ever take you away. We'd love you as much as we do Kathryn."

Kathryn beamed at him. She was bouncing slightly on her chair. Ruth was sitting next to Tadpole on the settee. Or he had been. When Massot mentioned adopting them, he'd jumped up and hugged her, squealing with delight. His cast clunked the back of the settee.

"Yes, yes, yes. I want to be adopted. I've wanted you as my mother ever since I came here." He hugged Ruth again and his cast clunked her on the back of her head. "Oh, I'm sorry. That won't make you not want me, will it?" Fear filled his eyes and voice.

"No, silly. That was an accident. I love you. I want

you to be my son just like Massot wants you to be his."
Ruth held him close.

"This is the best day ever." Tadpole jumped off her
lap and ran to hug Massot. "I've decided on the day I
want for my birthday."

"You have? Which one?" Massot placed his arm
around the boy.

"It's a real important decision, you know. I could
choose today since this is a real important day too. I get
me a mama and papa. But I'm gonna stick with the one
I thought up before."

"Well, are you going to tell us?" Kathryn asked with
a bounce.

"I asked Mrs. Blanche what the day was we got
brought here. She told me it were April sixth. That's
gonna be my birthday. We all got a whole new life that
day. Sort of like being born all over again."

Kathryn was bouncing even more. "I'm so excited.
I've always wanted a sister and brother."

Massot looked at Mae. Her face was white and her
eyes wide. He knelt down in front of her. "Mae, it's
okay if you don't want to. It's an offer. You can say no.
We thought you might like to be with your brother."

Ruth went to Mae's chair. She knelt beside it and
touched the girl's cheek, turning her face to her. "We
want what you want, Mae. If you want to stay here,
that's fine. We know how much you love Blanche.
You'll see lots of Tadpole and us. You can even come to
our house if you want to visit."

Tears slipped down Mae's face. She looked at
Tadpole, then Kathryn. Finally, she turned back to
Massot and shook her head.

"You want to stay here, Mae?" he asked.

She nodded.

He hugged her. "That's fine. We still love you. We'll be an aunt and uncle to you. There if you ever need us."

Mae gave a watery smile, then got up and went to her brother who looked a little confused.

"You're not getting adopted?" Tadpole asked.

She shook her head.

"It's okay, Tadpole," Ruth came and placed her hand on each child's shoulder. "Blanche loves her and she loves Blanche. That's not to say that she doesn't love you. It's more that Mae feels safest with Blanche. Am I right, Mae?"

The girl nodded.

Tadpole nodded back and hugged her. "I guess that's good then. I can still be your brother even if I'm living in the woods with my new family." He smiled at Massot and Ruth and turned his gaze on Kathryn. "Hey, I'm gonna have two sisters." He looked back at Ruth with mischief in his eyes. "How come you couldn't have had a boy?"

Kathryn and Mae both grabbed him and rubbed their knuckles over his head as he shouted in protest.

EPIOGUE

Ruth stood in her new nightgown in front of the windows that looked out over Stones Creek. She wasn't admiring the view. She was watching the door, waiting for it to open and her husband to enter.

The wedding had been wonderful. Kathryn and Mae were her bridesmaids. Tadpole and Newt Riverby stood up with Massot. Laura had Libby and Gema stand with her. Laura's sons, Eddie and Mark, were Hank's groomsmen. Red Dickerson stood next to Mark, just in case the boys acted out.

Cake and punch were enjoyed after the ceremony. Hank and Laura were going on a honeymoon to Denver for a week. Eddie would remain at the House, while Mark was spending the time with Red and Gema at Hawk's Wing Ranch.

Kathryn and Tadpole wouldn't move to Massot's house for a few days. Ruth and Massot wanted a few days by themselves. They'd decided to take a honeymoon in the winter when Massot wouldn't be so busy. It would also give them time to figure out where they wanted to go. Ruth had protested, saying travel would be too expensive. Massot had taken her to the bank and shown her his bank book. She'd given in and was planning on enjoying searching for a place or places they might want to go.

The door opened and her husband came in. He was in a nightshirt. They stared at each other. Massot finally approached and wrapped his arms around her.

"A long time ago, I asked a woman to marry me. She said I'd never be able to give her what she wanted if I was only a carpenter." His voice was rougher than usual. "I left and came to Stones Creek figuring I'd never marry. That I'd never be enough for any woman. Then you came to town.

"I was hesitant to ask to court you, thinking I wasn't enough. Then you were reluctant and I thought I still wasn't good enough."

Ruth put her fingers on his lips. "It was never you. It was always my fears and protecting myself from them. With you I always felt safe. When you rescued Kathryn, she was so brave. She helped me understand that I shouldn't hold on to the past, thinking that made me safe. She reminded me of a verse and it made me think of you.

"He will cover you with His feathers; you will take refuge under His wings. His faithfulness will be a protective shield. It's Psalm 91:4. I know I can take refuge under His wings and also under yours."

"I'll always protect you and the children. Together we'll all be sheltered under His protective wings."

Massot lowered his mouth to hers, kissing her deeply. Then he scooped her into his arms and carried her to their bed.

Much later, Ruth snuggled against his side, her head on his chest. The sensation of feathers brushing over them made her eyes open. She smiled and kissed

Massot softly on his chest. The arm around her tightened and she knew she was safe, protected, and exactly where she was supposed to be.

CHARACTER LIST HIS PROTECTIVE WINGS

With the growth of Stones Creek and the many people who live there, I've decided a list of the main characters might be of interest and beneficial to the reader. Only the major characters are listed. This list includes those who appear in the Stones Creek Series and first book of Stones Creek Ladies of Sanctuary House Series. Children's ages reflect their age at the end of the book.

Sanctuary House Ladies and their children.

Gema Volkovichna Dickerson
Blanche Basking
    Oswald Basking (Ozzie) - Blanche's son (13)
    William Basking (Will) - Blanche's son (11)
    Nancy Basking - Blanche's daughter (8)
    John Basking - Blanche's son (6)
Laura Duffle -Engaged to Hank Johnson
    Edward Duffle (Eddie) - Laura's son (9)
    Mark Duffle - Laura's son (7)
Ruth Naylor
    Kathryn Naylor - Ruth's daughter (12)
Cora Sepal Levine
    Susan Sepal - Cora's daughter (3)
Libby Trembly
    Jack Tanner - Foster son to Libby (18 months)
    Arleta Tanner - Foster daughter to Libby (18 months)
    Boone (12)
    Mae (10)
    Tadpole (8)

Other Main Characters

Hawk Conner - Owner Hawk's Wing Ranch

Hank Johnson - Barber
Noah Preston - Preacher, Gunsmith
Flora Potter
Sally Rife
   Nina - Sally's daughter (3)
Ada (14)

Stones Creek residents

Eli Steele - Doctor in Stones Creek
Leah Steele - Wife to Eli
Lincoln Pierce (Linc) - Foreman of Chasing R Ranch
Elenora Pierce (Norie) - Linc's wife, daughter of Wes Chase, owner of Chasing R Ranch
Wesley Chase (Wes) - Owner of Chasing R Ranch, Norie's father
Ben Cutler - Owner of Cutler's General Store
Sara Cutler - Ben's wife
   Seth Cutler - Son of Ben and Sara (11)
   Abigail Cutler (Abby) - Daughter of Ben and Sara (9)
   Clayton Cutler - Son of Ben and Sara (3)
Newt Riverby - Sheriff
Myra Riverby - Sheriff Newt's wife
   Troy Hope - Myra's son (5)
McIlroy - Blacksmith
Chloe McIlroy - Blacksmith's wife
   Duncan Ashburn (Dunc) - Chloe's Son (14)
     Penelope Ashburn (Lil-Pen) - Chloe's daughter (5)
Thomas Wilson - Ex-slave
Almeda Wilson - Ex-slave, Thomas's wife
Spike Hunter - Head wrangler on Chasing R Ranch

Doris Hunter - Housekeeper on Chasing R Ranch, Spike's wife
Vernie Preston - Noah Preston's wife
Nugget Nate Ryder - Uncle of Ben Cutler
Penny Ryder - Nate's wife
Garfield Steele - Eli's father
Chalmers Jehosaphat Ritter (CJ) - Banker
Arty Massot - Carpenter
Forsyth Franklin Fredrick Farnsworth the Fourth (Four) - Lawyer

~~~~~

I hope you enjoyed **His Protective Wings**. Please take a moment to leave a review on Amazon. For independently publishing authors like myself, the reviews are extremely valuable in getting our work noticed. If you take just a few minutes you could help someone else find their next favorite book.

You can post a review right from your Kindle or Kindle app. Just scroll past the end of the book. The form will pop up. Although Amazon says they require 20 words they will post it with fewer. You can pad your review with the title of the book and author name.

If you've missed any of my books or want to read more of them, head to my Amazon Author page. http://amazon.com/author/sophiedawson

Here are ways you can keep up with my sales and upcoming releases.

Sign up for my newsletter https://mailchi.mp/449be73f3465/sophiedawsonnewsletter

Join my Sophie's Reader Friends group on Facebook. https://www.facebook.com/groups/139425236751751/

Thank you.
  Sophie

www.ingramcontent.com/pod-product-compliance
Lightning Source LLC
Chambersburg PA
CBHW052002220626
47052CB00004B/1062